PURRFECT MURDER

THE MYSTERIES OF MAX 1

NIC SAINT

PURRFECT MURDER

The Mysteries of Max 1

Edited by Chereese Graves

www.nicsaint.com

Give feedback on the book at: info@nicsaint.com

facebook.com/nicsaintauthor
@nicsaintauthor

Third Edition

Printed in the U.S.A

PURRFECT MURDER

Sometimes it takes a cat to catch a killer

There's something special about Max. He may look like your regular ginger flabby tabby, but unlike most tabbies he can communicate with his human, reporter for the Hampton Cove Gazette Odelia Poole. Max takes a keen interest in the goings-on in their small town, by snooping around with his best friends Dooley, a not-too-bright ragamuffin, and Harriet, a gorgeous white Persian. Their regular visits to the police station, the barbershop and the doctor's office provide them with those precious and exclusive scoops that have made Odelia the number one reporter in town.

But when suddenly the body of a bestselling writer is discovered buried in the last Long Island outhouse, and a new policeman arrives in town to solve the murder, it looks like things are about to change in Hampton Cove. Detective Chase Kingsley doesn't take kindly to nosy reporters like Odelia snooping around 'his' crime scene or interviewing 'his' suspects. And to make matters worse, he's got a cat of his own: Brutus, a buff bully, who likes to lay down the law. Soon Brutus isn't just restricting access to all of Max's usual haunts, but he's getting awfully friendly with Harriet, threatening to break up the band.

Now it's all Odelia, Max and Dooley can do to try and solve the murder, in spite of Detective Kingsley's and Brutus's protestations, and show the overbearing cop and his bullyragging feline how things are done in Hampton Cove. Will Odelia find the killer before Detective Kingsley does? And will Max prevent Brutus from moving in on his territory and taking over the town? Find out in *Purrfect Murder*, the first book in the popular *Mysteries of Max* series.

CHAPTER 1

I lifted one eyelid and smiled approvingly at the sun bathing the room in its golden hue. It was eight o'clock in the morning and high time for an extended nap, but first I needed to see my human off to work. As usual, Odelia had a hard time throwing off the blanket of sleep and facing the world. She was still in bed, even though her alarm clock had gone off, and I'd alerted her to the fact that a new day was dawning by meowing plaintively and as loudly as I possibly could, pawing the wardrobe door in the process. She'd thrown a throw pillow at me, so I knew she got the message.

It wouldn't be long now. Odelia might hate getting up in the morning, but eventually she inevitably does, so I stretched and rolled over onto my back.

I have to admit I really lucked out when I was selected by Odelia to become her pet eight years ago, when she picked me out of the litter and decided I was a keeper. Odelia is not only one of the nicest and most decent humans a cat could ever hope to get, but she's also very generous when it comes to distributing the kibble and other goodies. She keeps my

1

bowl filled to the rim, and frequently adds a tasty wet food surprise to the mix.

My name is Max, by the way, and as you might have guessed I'm a feline. A male feline. Some of my friends call me fat, but that's a vicious lie. I'm big-boned. All the tabbies in my family are. It's genetics. And, just like my brothers and sisters, I'm blorange. A blend of orange and blond.

Today was going to be a special day. I could feel it in my bones. Yes, my big bones. But it wasn't merely my intuition. Harriet, the white Persian belonging to Odelia's parents who live next door, told me last night that a new cop had moved to Hampton Cove. And if she hadn't told me I would have found out for myself, for there was a new cat on the block. A nasty brute aptly called Brutus. Black as coal, built like Tom Brady, and with evil green eyes, Brutus barged into our midnight meeting in Hampton Cove Park last night, announcing he was now in charge of all the public spaces in Hampton Cove, on account of the fact that his owner was a cop. I called it delusions of grandeur, and in response Brutus demonstrated the sharpness of his claws by stripping a nice piece of bark from my favorite tree. Gulp!

Not a cat you want to rumble with, in other words. And if his owner was made of the same cloth, the town of Hampton Cove was in for a rough ride.

"Hey, Max," Odelia's voice rang out as she descended the stairs.

"Over here," I said, giving her a wave from my position on the couch.

She plunked herself down next to me and gave my belly a tickle. She was still dressed in pink PJs, rubbing the sleep from her eyes with one hand while she rubbed my belly with the other. In response, I purred contentedly.

Odelia is slim and trim, with shoulder-length blond hair and big eyes the color of seaweed that always sparkle with the light of intelligence. She grimaced when a ray of sunshine hit her face. "Wow, too much too soon."

"Not really," I said. "Sun's been up since before seven, sleepyhead."

"You don't have to rub it in," she said, getting up with a groan. "I was up late last night working on a piece about that sinkhole on Hayes Road."

She shuffled into the kitchen and started up the coffeemaker while I tripped after her, then hopped onto one of the kitchen counter stools so we could continue our conversation. Oh, didn't I mention it? Odelia belongs to that rare kind of human who can converse with cats. Not that she's Doctor Dolittle or something, but she comes from a long line of women with a strong affinity with the feline species. As far as I understand it, her foremothers were witches, at a time when being a witch was a surefire way of getting burned at the stake. And even though that witchy streak has diminished over the generations, the women in her family can talk to cats, and do so to their heart's content. Odelia even claims her ancestors used to turn themselves into cats and back. No idea if that's true but it's pretty cool.

I glanced at my bowl, and saw it was still half full, which was better than half empty, so I returned my attention to Odelia, who was pouring cornflakes into her own bowl. Yikes. How she can eat that stuff, I do not know.

"Did you hear the latest?" I asked, draping my tail around my buttocks.

"No, what's that?"

"There's a new cop in town."

This seemed to interest her, for she looked up from her cereal. "Oh?"

"Some hotshot who calls himself Chase Kingsley. Used to work for the NYPD."

"The NYPD? So what is he doing in Hampton Cove?"

I shrugged. Yes, cats can shrug, though it's hard to notice with all the hair. "Beats me. All I know is that people are saying he might succeed your uncle as chief of police."

Odelia frowned. "That's impossible. Uncle Alec is only…" She frowned some more. "Actually I have no idea how old he is."

"He's older than your mother," I supplied.

"Yeah, but not old enough to retire, surely."

"Maybe he wants to take early retirement?"

"I'll have to ask him," she said, making a mental note of this.

Odelia works for the *Hampton Cove Gazette* as a reporter, and I give her the odd scoop now and then. Since cats are pretty much all over the place, I've been able to provide her with a steady stream of breaking news over the years, ranging from that rat infestation at Dough Knot Bakery, to the milk spill at the dairy farm. Cats were all over that one, as you can imagine.

This has given Odelia's career quite a boost, and given her the reputation of a hard-nosed reporter. Her editor often asks her where she gets her information, but she's been diligently protecting her sources—*moi*. If word ever got out that her sources all have whiskers, a furry tail and a propensity for licking their own patootie, she'd probably be front-page news herself.

"I should probably do an interview with this Chase Kingsley."

She took a tentative sip from her coffee and perked up. It's something I've never understood about humans. How they can drink that horrible brew. I jumped up on this kitchen counter once to have a lick at the stuff, and I couldn't believe how horrible it tasted. I'll take a piece of chicken liver every time.

"You should. I hear he's one of those hunkishly handsome guys."

She looked up at this. "Hunkishly handsome?"

"And single, if the word on the street is to be believed. At least that's what Harriet told me." I shook my head disgustedly. "Probably one of those playboy types who goes around hitting on every woman in sight."

"I'll bet he's not," said Odelia, taking the next seat.

"Oh, yes, he is. If Harriet is mooning over Chase Kingsley you can rest assured he's a regular playboy. She's always falling for that kind of guy."

"She can't fall for that kind of guy," said Odelia, making a funny face. "Harriet is a cat, Max. Cats don't fall for humans. It's simply not possible."

"Oh, yes, they do. Cats fall for humans all the time, only not for the same reason humans fall for other humans. When we fall for one of you it's because you provide us with a great home, great food and great cuddles."

"And why does Harriet think this Chase Kingsley provides all of that?"

"Because he's got a cat of his own. A nasty brute called Brutus. I met him last night and he's a real piece of work. And if his owner is anything like him, we've got another thing coming in this town. Do you know what he told me?"

She took a swig from her coffee. "What?"

I lowered my voice. "He only eats meat. No kibble. Can you believe it?"

She laughed. "Sounds to me like you're jealous, Max."

"Hey, I'm the least jealous cat in this town."

"Why does eating meat make Brutus a bad cat?"

"Because... who gives their cat only raw meat? It's simply not done!"

She nodded. "Who's got the money, right?"

"Exactly. You certainly don't." If this came across as a

barb, I didn't mean it. I totally get how Odelia can't afford to feed me filet mignon every day. Not on a reporter's salary.

But if I expected her to be offended, I was mistaken. Instead, a keen look had appeared in her eyes. "Do you think this Chase Kingsley is rich?"

"I doubt it. A cop? Rich? Highly unlikely."

"Maybe he comes from money?"

I shook my head. "I don't think so. If he did, either Brutus or Harriet would have told me. The guy's a regular blabbermouth, and so is Harriet, as you well know."

"Know what?" asked a voice from the door.

CHAPTER 2

*O*h, darn it. That's the problem with cats. They tread so softly you never hear them coming until they're already upon you.

"Hey, Harriet," I said when the white Persian strode into the kitchen. As usual, she was looking a little haughty, her nose in the air. Harriet seems to feel she descends from the Queen of Sheba. Or at least the Queen of Hampton Cove.

"We were just saying how well-informed you always are," said Odelia.

Nice save! "Yeah, how you always seem to know everything about everybody," I added sweetly.

She smiled at this. You might be surprised that cats can smile, but they can. Again, it's the fur. It obscures many of our facial tics. "It's true," she said complacently. "I do know everything about everybody all of the time."

"Max was just telling me about this new cop in town," said Odelia.

"Chase," she said, nodding. "A real dreamboat."

"Oh, my goodness," I groaned. "Here we go again."

"No, but he is," she insisted. "He's just about the most

handsome human male I've ever laid eyes on, and I've laid eyes on my fair share of handsome humans over the years."

Listening to Harriet, you would almost think she's a human herself, which is a phenomenon quite common amongst cats. They spend so much time with humans they get confused. It's called cross-species confusion. It's a thing. It really is. At least I think it is. "If he's as handsome as Brutus, I can tell you that you're blind, Harriet," I said now. "That man isn't handsome. He's scary."

"There's nothing scary about Brutus," she said huffily. "He's a fine cat."

"He's a bully, that's what he is, and I don't like him one bit. Barging in here as if he owns the place." Then suddenly it dawned on me what Harriet had said. I narrowed my eyes at her. "How would you know what Chase Kingsley looks like? Did you see him?"

"Of course I did." Her face took on a beatific quality. "He looks lovely when he sleeps. Like a buff angel."

Odelia emitted an incredulous laugh. "You watched him sleep?"

"Of course. I walked Brutus home last night and he invited me in. Who was I to say no? Especially when it gave me the chance to get a glimpse of the new cop in town. And I have to say Chase Kingsley is everything Brutus said he was and more." She emitted a giggle. "He sleeps in his boxers. No PJs."

If I could have, I would have covered my ears with my paws. "Please, Harriet. Let's keep it clean."

"He sleeps in his boxers?" asked Odelia.

Harriet gave her tail a studious lick. "Boxers... and nothing more. *Très* cute."

I held up my paw. "Enough already. Brutus is a bully and I'm pretty sure so is his master. Or have you forgotten that pets and their owners often share distinctive traits?"

"Oh, please. Odelia's blond and you're orange."

"I'm blorange, which is almost the same thing as blond."

"I'm sure that's not even a real color."

"It is a color," I assured her. "It's strawberry blond, with gold rose hues."

"You're crazy," Harriet sighed, shaking her snowy white fur.

"Hey, no name calling, please," warned Odelia. "Now tell me more about this new cop. Where does he live?"

"He's staying with your uncle at the moment. Until he finds his own place."

Odelia's eyes were positively glittering with interest. So I gave her a warning scowl. "Don't listen to Harriet. The guy is a bully. Waltzing into town as if he owns the place. Leaving his repulsive pee all over the place."

Odelia frowned. "Leaving his pee? You mean Chase Kingsley is a public urinator? That's not right for a cop. Or anyone else for that matter."

"Not Kingsley, Brutus. Though I wouldn't put it past his human either."

"How would you know? You haven't even met the guy," Harriet challenged.

"I just know these things. I'm a great judge of character."

"You're simply jealous because both Brutus and Chase are big, butch males and you're not."

"They're bullies," I pointed out. "There's a distinction."

She turned to Odelia. "You should snap him up now, Odelia, if you want to have a shot at him. He's bound to become very popular very soon."

This appeared to be one bridge too far for Odelia, though. "I have no intention whatsoever to snap anyone up," she said, her smile vanishing. "The only reason I'm asking is because I'll need to write a piece about the guy."

"I'm sure Uncle Alec will drop by the newspaper today to

introduce him," Harriet said, then lowered her gaze. "So you better make sure you're dressed to the nines, Odelia. Remember what they say about first impressions."

"Odelia doesn't have to dress up to make a great first impression," I said. "And what's more, I don't see why she has to make a great first impression in the first place. It's not as if she's even remotely interested in the man, is she?" I gave Odelia a pointed look, but she chose to ignore me. Never a good sign!

"I can always make an extra effort," she said instead, dragging her fingers through her long blond tresses and shaking them out until they fanned out across her shoulders. Uh-oh.

"Why would you want to dress up for that cop?" I asked, alarmed.

She laughed. "You're overreacting, Max. I just want to make sure I look presentable for our first meeting. I'll probably spend a considerable amount of time with the man, working closely together as I have with Uncle Alec."

That was true enough. As a reporter, she often sat together with the Chief to thresh out the details of some case he was working on.

She now rose from the chair and drained the final dregs from her cup, then transferred it to the sink and gave it a good rinse. "Think I'll go and get ready, you guys." She winked at Harriet. "Don't want to be late for work."

Harriet purred approvingly. The moment Odelia had disappeared upstairs, Harriet gave me a supercilious look. "See? She likes him already. That's women's intuition for you."

"Oh, boy," I muttered. I had a bad feeling about this. Odelia hooking up with this cop? No way. Imagine they hit it off. Next thing they'd be moving in together, which meant I'd have to share my space with Brutus. Not only my space, but my food, too. And my extra special place at the foot of the bed!

"Trouble in paradise?" asked Harriet sweetly. Too sweetly for my taste.

"I can't share my home with Brutus, Harriet," I said, shaking my head nervously. "I can't live with that bully!"

"I told you, he's not a bully, Max. Brutus is simply a stickler for discipline. Just like his human, I would imagine. They're both cops, not bullies."

But I wasn't fooled. Last night Brutus had peed all over my favorite tree, just to taunt me. When I complained, he pointed out that Hampton Cove Park and its trees were part of the public domain, and as such off limits to cats that weren't law enforcement like him. If I wanted to mark a tree as my own, I would have to do it in my own backyard, not the park. It was an awfully narrow interpretation of the Hampton Cove penal code, I felt.

"He practically chased us out of the park last night!" I cried.

"He did nothing of the kind. He simply pointed out that we're not supposed to view the park as part of our personal territory."

"He said I should stick to my backyard from now on!"

"Well, isn't your backyard big enough for you? And if you're so desperate for space you can take a tinkle in my backyard, too, Max. All right? *Mi jardin es su jardin.*"

"I don't even know what that means," I grumbled. Or actually I did. It meant that from now on, this town wasn't ours anymore. This big brute Brutus had taken over.

"Hey, you guys," a voice spoke from the living room. "Where are you?"

"Over here, Dooley!" I called out.

The Ragamuffin came tripping over. "Oh, hey," he said.

Dooley is Odelia's grandmother's cat, and also my best

NIC SAINT

friend. He's a small, grayish-beigeish, fluffy hairball, and divides his time between Odelia's home and her parents' home right next door.

"What were you guys talking about?" he asked.

"The new cat in town," I said.

Dooley's eyes widened. "There's a new cat in town?"

"Brutus," Harriet said. "Remember from last night? We met at the park?"

"He told you not to rub yourself against your favorite tree," I added.

"Oh, that Brutus," he said, his face clearing. "What about him?"

"Harriet seems to think he's something special," I said. "While I think he's simply bad news."

Dooley shivered. "I thought he was very intense."

"Thank you, Dooley," I said. "Brutus *is* intense."

Harriet didn't agree, of course. "Perhaps it's because he has taken on so much responsibility. That kind of pressure can weigh on a cat."

"What responsibility!" I cried. "He's just a cat!"

"He does have great fur, though," said Dooley.

I turned to him. "What?!"

"That's raw meat for you," said Harriet, a little enviously.

"He gets raw meat?" asked Dooley, surprised.

"*Only* raw meat," I agreed grudgingly.

"No wonder he's so buff and fit!" said Dooley.

"He is buff and fit, isn't he?" gushed Harriet. "He's simply dreamy."

"He's a musclebound bully," I grumbled.

"Who is a musclebound bully?" asked Odelia, stepping into the kitchen. She'd showered and dressed and looked cute as a button in a flowery summer dress that revealed quite a bit of cleavage and a lot of leg. My jaw dropped. If this was the way she was going to meet Chase Kingsley I might as well welcome Brutus into our home right now. The guy would fall for her like a ton of bricks. I just knew he would. No one could resist my human when she was all fresh-faced and cute as a button like this.

"Brutus," I said, in a last-ditch effort to stop this terrible ordeal from taking place. "Like his master, he's a muscle-bound bully who's addicted to meat."

"You can't be addicted to meat," Dooley laughed. "It's an essential component of a well-balanced diet. And what's essential can't be addictive."

I scowled at my friend. "Thank you, Dr. Phil."

Dooley blinked confusedly. "Who's Dr. Phil?"

"You guys better behave," said Odelia as she snatched her clutch from the counter and strode to the sliding glass door that leads into the backyard. She closed it. "Oh, and could you find out whatever you can about Mr. Kingsley?"

Now it was my turn to blink confusedly. "Anything?"

"Sure. The more I know about him, the better... for my article," she concluded lamely.

I saw an opportunity. An opportunity to dig up some dirt on this new supercop, so I nodded. "Of course. Absolutely."

"Great. See you later, sweethearts."

"See you later, Odelia," said Harriet.

"Have a wonderful day," said Dooley.

I didn't say anything. I was thinking hard how to stop my human from getting involved with this Brutus's human and making my worst nightmare come true!

We watched Odelia walk out the front door, then return five seconds later to grab her sunglasses from the hallway credenza, then return again to grab her smartphone, give us a goofy grin, a cheery wave, and pull the door shut.

"Oh, don't look so glum," said Harriet.

"You would look glum if you were about to be kicked out of your own home," I said gloomily.

"Brutus won't kick you out of your home."

"He will, too. First he kicked me out of the park, now he'll kick me out of my home. He's a natural born bully."

"He's not. He's simply... a natural born leader."

"And what does that make me? A natural born loser?"

Harriet merely grinned.

"Oh, I can see what's going on here," I said. "Odelia is getting involved with the new cop, and you're getting involved with the new cat in town. Is that how it is?"

She shrugged and sashayed in the direction of the pet flap. "Time for my beauty nap, fellas. See you later." And with a swish of her tail, she gracefully disappeared through the door and was gone.

"So who's Dr. Phil?" Dooley asked after a pause.

"Oh, Dooley," I sighed.

CHAPTER 3

I resisted the temptation to take a long nap on my favorite blanket, the one Odelia had put on the couch to protect it from my habit of digging my nails into any soft cover I encounter. I needed to check out this cop person first. If this Chase Kingsley decided to put the moves on my human and saddle me with Brutus, I needed to stop him dead in his tracks before that happened.

So I bade goodbye to Dooley and waddled out the pet flap and into the backyard. After sniffing at a couple of trees, just to make sure no one had trespassed on my domain, I set out along the road, slowly making my way into town. It didn't take long before I reached the police station. It's the place where cops like to gather to snack on glazed donuts and coffee before starting their job of catching bad people.

Not that there are a lot of bad people in Hampton Cove. In fact it's probably the most peaceful town on the South Shore. Apart from your occasional rowdy tourist collapsing on the beach or wrapping their car around a tree, it's a pretty peaceful little town, and we like to keep it that way.

I hurried across the road, narrowly being missed by a

speeding car, past the doctor's office where Odelia's dad Tex works, and the library, where her mom works as a librarian, and finally reached the town square, with the giant clock the mayor installed a couple of years ago and which has proved such a hit with locals and tourists alike, and then I was homing in on the police station.

A squat one-story building, it sports the words 'Hampton Cove Police Department' above the entrance. Behind those double doors, Dolores Peltz sits, presiding over the vestibule and always ready to take note of any complaint the citizenry might have. Since technically I wasn't part of the citizenry, and couldn't very well waltz in through the front door, I walked around back instead, and headed straight for the window of Uncle Alec's office, where I'd picked up many a private conversation over the years.

I hopped up onto the windowsill and once again praised Uncle Alec's good sense always to leave the window open a crack. Someone must have told him once that fresh air was good for him, and I could only agree wholeheartedly.

One peek inside the office of the good chief told me that I'd hit the jackpot. He was in there with a hunkish male I'd never seen before. His long limbs stretched out languidly, his athletic body casually draped across a chair, he was listening to Uncle Alec intently. He was definitely a handsome fella. He had one of those square jaws and chiseled faces that were all the rage with the ancient Greeks. A lock of dark brown hair dangled across his brow, his hair a little too long for a cop, which gave him a rebellious look.

His white cotton shirt was stretched taut over bulging chest muscles, and his arms were all biceps and triceps and whatnot and his belly was perfectly flat, unlike the big tummy Uncle Alec has going for himself. If I'd had to venture a guess, I'd have pegged the man in his early thirties, and never had the words 'ruggedly handsome' been a better description for a human male. Odelia was definitely in trouble, if my limited experience was anything to go on.

I hunkered down and pricked up my ears, hoping to find confirmation that this guy was, indeed, Chase Kingsley, and not simply a tourist filing a complaint about a stolen wallet, or a traveling salesman badgering the chief.

"So what do we know so far?" the guy was saying.

"I just called the coroner's office," said Uncle Alec, "and they told me they're expecting the results from the autopsy sometime this morning."

The Chief, a mainstay in this town for over thirty years, is the embodiment of law and order. He is also a very large man, easily twice as big as the man seated across from him. Everyone knows Alec Lip as a kind-hearted, fair-minded police officer, and never one to throw his (admittedly sizable) weight around. He likes to settle disputes with a smile and a kindly word, ever the courteous diplomat.

And then it dawned on me. Autopsy? Had someone died? I turned my antennae-like ears toward the window, my eyes narrowing in concentration.

"Good thing Adele Pun found the body. The poor guy might never have been found otherwise," said the one I assumed was Chase Kingsley.

"You're right about that, Chase," grunted the Chief.

Bingo! I stared at Brutus's owner, and couldn't resist uttering a growl.

"That body was never meant to be found, and if Mrs. Pun hadn't gone snooping around, the killer would have pulled off the perfect crime."

I blinked. Killer? Crime? Oh. My. God. They were talking about a murder!

"So how did Adele Pun discover the body?" asked Chase.

The Chief barked a curt, humorless laugh. "Well, that's a

writer for you, Chase. They will go sticking their noses where they don't belong."

At this, the Chief directed a long, lingering look at me, and I froze. Not that I minded too much. Uncle Alec is Odelia's uncle on her mother's side, after all, and I'm pretty sure he isn't aware of his sister and niece's big secret.

He looked away again, and continued his story. "She says she was using the outhouse a couple of days ago and suddenly started wondering where the product of her bowel movements went. Curious, she went and got herself a flashlight, to examine the bottom of the well, and shone it down into the abyss where generations of Hampton Covians have done their business."

"You should have been a poet, Chief," remarked Chase dryly.

"Thank you. Imagine her surprise when she discovered a laptop sticking out of the tranquil surface of the brown pool below. Being a writer, holed up at a writer's lodge, she naturally wondered what that laptop was doing there."

Chase made a face. "Don't tell me. She retrieved the laptop?"

The chief grinned. "She most certainly did. Though I have no idea how she did it. I imagine she used a shovel or a rake. Then she put the garden hose on the laptop and dumped it into a bucket of salt for three full days."

"And what? It booted up?"

"It sure did. Just goes to show those cheap laptops are a lot sturdier than you think. Reminds me never to spend two thousand bucks on a computer ever again."

"And that's how she discovered it was Paulo Frey's laptop."

"Yes, sir. None other than the elusive Mr. Frey."

"The missing writer."

"The missing writer," the Chief agreed.

I almost fell off the sill at this point. Paulo Frey was a famous novelist who'd gone missing some time last year. He'd been in the habit of renting the Writer's Lodge once a year, a fixed-up old cabin in the woods on the edge of Hampton Cove. The Lodge is very popular with writers, as there are no distractions out there, and they can work on their masterpieces undisturbed. There is even an old-fashioned outhouse, which for some reason seems to appeal to the writing classes. Many a writer has confessed that they got their best ideas whilst ensconced in that very outhouse and allowing nature to run its course. Weird but true.

Paulo Frey had been one of those writers who felt they could only write a decent novel while holed up at the Writer's Lodge, pecking away at his laptop. Until he'd mysteriously vanished. The owner of the lodge—Hetta Fried—a patron of the arts—had assumed he'd simply skipped town, but when he hadn't shown up in New York, his relatives had sounded the alarm.

The cabin had been thoroughly searched, but Mr. Frey hadn't left a trace, so no foul play was assumed. It wasn't as if he hadn't pulled a stunt like this before. Once he'd upped and left and had shown up six months later in Zimbabwe, living quietly in a hut in the jungle, trying to cure a severe case of writer's block. He was one of those eccentric writers.

"So Adele notified the police," said Chase.

"She notified me," the chief acknowledged. "At which point we decided to take a closer look at that outhouse."

Chase shook his head. "That must be the last outhouse on Long Island."

"It may very well be," Uncle Alec agreed. "It's garnered a lot of praise from writers. Supposed to give them ideas. Kinda like a wishing well. You drop in a nickel and you get to make a wish. Only here you drop in… well, something else."

"So when did you get the idea to dredge the well?"

"Well, at first we figured Frey had simply hurled his laptop into the pit in a fit of rage or something. Which would fit with the writer's block theory." The chief shifted his bulk, making his chair creak dangerously. "But after poking around in there for a bit, something else came bobbing up." He fixed Chase with a knowing glance. "An arm."

"Yikes."

"Yeah. So we called in a cesspool pumping service and found—"

"Paulo Frey."

"Along with all of his stuff, stuffed into three Louis Vuitton suitcases. All packed and ready to go... nowhere. Looks like whoever killed him wanted to make it look like he skipped town, while he was actually down there all along."

"I wouldn't like to be the medical examiner on this one," said Chase, wrinkling his nose.

"You said it," said the Chief, shaking his head. "This is one messy business."

"When will you know more?"

The Chief checked the clock over the door. It was one of those clocks that wouldn't have looked out of place in a classroom. "Shouldn't be long now. We don't get a lot of homicides here in Hampton Cove, so they're giving this their highest priority. I'm expecting a call before lunch." He patted the desk. "So what about it, Chase? Are you ready to work your first Hampton Cove homicide case?"

Chase grinned. "Throwing me in at the deep end, huh, Chief?"

"Best way to learn, buddy."

"What better way indeed?"

At this point in the conversation, I hopped down from the windowsill and landed gracefully on all fours on the flagged floor below. I'd heard enough. A homicide! In Hampton Cove! This was a scoop that needed to be on the front page

20

of the next edition of the *Hampton Cove Gazette*. Pronto! And who better to break the story to our loyal readership than star reporter Odelia Poole herself? This would cement her reputation as the town's best-informed reporter. Wait till I told her about this. She'd be over the moon!

And wait was exactly what I had to do, for as I made my way to the street, I found my passage blocked by a stocky, burly black cat with evil green eyes. It was, of course, Brutus!

"Snooping around, are we, Max?" he asked in a sneering manner. At that moment he suddenly reminded me of Draco Malfoy, Harry Potter's nemesis.

Oh, dear. This was exactly what I needed right now. Not!

"Step aside, Brutus," I told him. "This is none of your business."

But Brutus didn't make a move to let me pass. Instead, he walked right up to me and got in my face. "If anyone is getting involved in stuff that isn't his business, it's you, Max. I saw you, you know, spying on Chief Lip and Chase. So that's how you do things in this town, huh? You're Odelia Poole's personal spy. I knew there was a reason she was always getting the best scoops. And now I know her secret. Wait till I tell Chase all about this!"

A chill suddenly settled around the base of my spine. "How are you going to do that, Brutus? You can't talk to your human like I can talk to mine."

Oh, crap. Had I just said that? Bad Max!

He grinned evilly, like Bruce the shark from that fish movie Odelia likes to watch when she's babysitting one of her cousins.

"So you *can* talk to your humans," he said slowly. "I thought as much. I only arrived yesterday, but already I've heard the rumors this Odelia Poole person is a little... shall we say weird? And now you've confirmed my suspicions."

"You still can't do anything with that information," I said.

My claws were itching to get a piece of him, but I restrained myself. I may be big, but that doesn't mean I'm all lean muscle like Brutus and Chase. My bulk mainly consists of, um, well, love handles. Lots and lots of love handles.

"Maybe I can't talk to my human," he conceded, "but I can make your life a lot more difficult. I can prevent you from snooping around and listening to conversations that aren't intended for your spying ears."

Horrified, I cried, "You can't do that!"

"Oh, yes, I can," he said, that nasty grin still firmly in place. He reared up to his full height, puffing up his chest like the bully that he was. "Listen up, Max. From now on the police station is off limits to you and your buddies."

"What?! You have no right!"

"Oh, yes, I do. Chase is the law in this town now, which, by extension, makes me the law, too. So I can do whatever I want and there's not a thing you can do about it."

"It doesn't work like that! It's not because your human is a cop that you're also a cop. That just doesn't make sense!"

"I can assure you that's exactly how it works, Max."

"No, it doesn't. Harriet's human is a doctor. That doesn't make her capable of performing brain surgery, does it? And, and…" I cast around wildly. "Dooley's human is this town's biggest gossip. That doesn't mean he's a gossip, too." Oh, wait, actually it did. Dooley is a pretty big gossip. But that was neither here nor there. "The point I'm trying to make here is that you're not a cop, Brutus. Cats simply can't be cops."

"Well, you can't, obviously," he scoffed. "You're not trained to uphold the law. I, on the other hand, am. Chase used to be the NYPD's biggest and baddest detective, and I learned a lot from watching him in action."

"That's just a load of—"

"Hey!" Brutus yelled, holding up a warning paw, claws

extended. "Watch it, pal. You want me to arrest you for contempt of cop? No? Didn't think so!"

"Contempt of cop? That's not even a thing!"

"I'm sure it is," he said, giving his nose a lick.

"And I'm sure it isn't. You're making this up on the spot."

I tried to sidestep the overbearing cat, but he got in my face again, and hissed, "You're not trespassing again, Max. This is your final warning."

"Oh? And what are you going to do about it?" I challenged him, my tail rearing up and puffing up while I arched my back menacingly.

"Don't make me fight you, Max," he said in a low, menacing voice. "You don't want me to hurt you. I'm warning you."

I backed down. What? Have you ever stared into the slitted eyes of the meanest, biggest, nastiest cat you've ever seen? Let me tell you, it's scary!

"This was your final warning," he growled, and casually displayed three razor-sharp claws and gave me a mock punch on the shoulder.

I gulped. Those claws looked very sharp indeed. So I decided not to get into a fight with this cat. I needed to figure out how to deal with him, but brute force wasn't exactly my forte. That was obviously his department.

"Have it your way, Brutus," I finally said.

"Always," he said with a smug smile. "That's something you will learn soon enough, Max. You and those other furballs that inhabit this silly little town."

"Hampton Cove is not a silly little town!"

He merely grinned, and stalked off in the direction of the police station, swinging his tail like a baton.

Still shaking from the adrenaline, I started heading for the *Hampton Cove Gazette*. Boy, did I have news for Odelia!

CHAPTER 4

*B*efore going to the paper, Odelia decided to pass by her dad's doctor's office first. She wanted to check on Gran, who'd been feeling a little under the weather lately. She walked into the waiting room. As usual, there were already half a dozen patients patiently waiting to be called into her father's examination room. Tex Poole had been a popular family doctor for more than twenty years, and was well-respected and well-liked by all.

She nodded a greeting to the small gathering, and quickly walked up to the reception desk, and was relieved to find her grandmother seated behind it, reading glasses perched on the tip of her nose, tongue sticking out of her mouth as she deftly handled the phone and the appointments book.

"Gran," she said happily. "I'm so glad to see you're okay."

"Why wouldn't I be okay?" asked the white-haired old lady crustily.

"I heard you were feeling a little under the weather last night."

The old lady lifted her chin mutinously. "Who told you

24

that? That kind of information is strictly confidential. That's between my physician and me."

"Well, your physician is my dad," she said. "So…"

"That doesn't give him the right to go blabbing about my private affairs," Gran grumbled. "I'll have to have a word with that man."

Odelia laughed. "He didn't blab about anything, Gran. Mom told me last night you weren't feeling well after dinner, and that you went to bed early."

"Poppycock. I've never felt better and don't let anyone tell you different."

"I'm just glad to see you're fine." The last thing she wanted was to get into a fight with the feisty old lady, especially in front of half a dozen of her dad's patients.

"I just had an upset tummy, that's all. Nothing to get all worked up about."

Odelia stared at her. "You don't think it was my dessert, do you?"

She was the one who made dessert last night. Even though she lived alone, she still went home for dinner with her family most nights. It didn't make much sense to cook for herself when she was just one person. She and Mom took turns cooking, with Gran chipping in from time to time. Last night had been Mom's turn. She'd made grilled tuna, with Odelia providing dessert.

But Gran waved her hand. "Don't even think about it. That dessert was perfectly fine. I simply love your chocolate pudding. Now state your business."

She smiled. "Just checking up on you, Gran."

"This is a doctor's office, young lady, and we've got a lot of sick people waiting, so if you're not sick or dying, please move along. No dillydallying."

"Sure thing," she said with a laugh. "Have a nice day."

25

"Oh, I most definitely will," Gran said, then hollered, "Next!"

She passed into the street feeling better already. The old lady might be feisty, but she was also vulnerable at her age, and she was glad to know she was fine. Next stop was the newspaper, and she'd just walked into her own small office when Max came tripping up.

"It's about time," the big orange kitty grumbled. "I thought you'd never show up."

"And a good day to you too, Max," she said as she took a seat.

"Oh, boy," said Max, hopping onto the desk. "Have I got news for you!"

This morning ritual of theirs wasn't unusual. Max might get most of his information from other cats, whom he met on his nocturnal excursions, but he often made a quick trip around town during the daytime as well, to see if he couldn't pick up some nice little tidbits of news here or there. The police station, especially, often rewarded them both with some great stories fit to print.

She needed to vet them, of course, and run them by her editor, Dan Goory, who'd been running the paper since before Odelia was born, but he trusted her, and never pressed her for her sources, knowing she wouldn't reveal them anyway. And even if she did, she knew he wouldn't believe her.

The weird thing about her uncanny knack was that it only seemed to work on cats. She'd tried talking to dogs, but they simply stared at her dumbly, then continued licking their tushies or chasing their tails as if she hadn't spoken.

"Spill, please," she said as she took her notebook and sat with pencil poised while Max spilled the latest news straight from the chief of police's mouth. But when he'd finished his tale, she still hadn't jotted down a word, too shocked at what he'd told her. "Paulo Frey? Murdered?" she gasped.

"Yep, and found at the bottom of the Writer's Lodge cesspit. The medical examiner is trying to figure out what killed him and Chief Alec is expecting his report some time this morning. Only trouble is…"

"What?" she asked anxiously as she feverishly started taking notes. She needed to confirm all of this with her uncle, of course, but this was one heck of a story.

"I've been told not to go near the police station again."

She looked up, startled. "What? Who told you?"

"Brutus," he said bitterly. "That big brute who belongs to Chase Kingsley. He's been throwing his weight around ever since he arrived in town. He says the police station is off limits to me and my friends from now on."

She immediately recognized this for what it was: a clear and present danger to her job. If Max wasn't allowed to sneak up to Uncle Alec's window and snap up any and all snippets of information, she was out of a very valuable news source. Not that her uncle was secretive, or unwilling to share, but his niece wasn't the first person he ran to when he had important information to impart. Though he'd gotten used to her finding out anyway.

"Listen, Max," she said earnestly. "Don't let this cat boss you around. Tell him he's got no business telling other cats where they can and cannot go."

"That's what I told him! But he threatened me with violence if I didn't do what he said." He sighed. "I told you. He's a regular bully."

"This simply won't do," she said, shaking her head. "Who does he think he is, bossing others around like that?"

"He seems to feel he's the new cop in town."

"We'll see about that," said Odelia, and rose from behind her desk.

"Where are you going, Odelia?" asked Dan from his own office as she strode past.

"The police station!" she yelled back. "I've got a scoop!" She quickly stuck her head into the old editor's office and grinned at him. Then she said the words she'd wanted to say for a very long time. "Stop the presses, Dan. And hold the front page. I've got the scoop to end all scoops."

"Oh? What is it?"

Her eyes glittered with excitement. "A murder."

"Murder in Hampton Cove!" cried the editor, his glasses almost falling from his face as he shot up from behind his desk. "No way!"

"Yes, way," she confirmed. "I'll be back in a jiffy so hold that front page."

"I sure will," he said, a look of happiness on his kindly hobbit face. The news that a murder had taken place might appall regular folk, but reporters aren't regular folk, of course. To them, murder and mayhem are like music to their ears.

Odelia purposefully set foot for the police station, and thought about what Max said about this Brutus character. It was time that Chase Kingsley taught his cat a few lessons in common courtesy. You didn't just waltz into town and start bossing people around. That simply was not done!

The police station was only half a block away from the *Gazette*, and it didn't take her more than a few minutes to get there and walk into the vestibule. Dolores gave her a little wave as she marched past the woman's desk and through the short corridor to her uncle Alec's office.

She and the police chief had developed a good working relationship over the years. He knew how important it was that the public be informed about the goings-on in their town, and that Odelia had a unique skill set that made her well-placed to report on those goings-on. She knew stuff before anyone else did, and he helped her fill in the gaps and occasionally even enlisted her to help him on any small investigation he had running.

It also helped that he was her uncle, of course, and often sat down for dinner with them. Odelia's mom had more or less taken him under her wing after his wife died, and he was now pretty much a fixture at the house, and enjoyed their cooking almost more than Odelia's dad himself.

So she simply barged into his office without knocking and said, "Hey, Uncle Alec. What's all this I'm hearing about Paulo Frey being found at the bottom of a cesspit?"

Only now did she notice that there was a third person in the office, seated across from the Chief. He was tall and lanky, with chiseled features and clear blue eyes. Those eyes now swiveled to her and took her in with a sharp look.

Uncle Alec had risen. "Um, Odelia, this is Chase Kingsley. Chase, this is my niece Odelia Poole. She's a reporter with the *Hampton Cove Gazette*."

The detective's eyes were still fixed on her, and judging from the expression on his face he wasn't happy. "How the heck did you find out about Paulo Frey?"

The Chief gave a feeble smile. "Odelia has her sources, don't you, honey?"

"I sure have," she said, taking a seat in the other chair, her notebook poised on her lap. "So is it true that you found all of his suitcases, his laptop and all of his belongings buried down there along with the body?"

Detective Kingsley shook his head. "Unbelievable," he grunted.

She snapped her head up. "What's unbelievable?"

"The way information gets leaked!" he said, incensed.

"The people of Hampton Cove have a right to know what's going on in their town, Mr. Kingsley," she said. "So I suggest you get used to it."

"It's *Detective* Kingsley to you," he grumbled.

"We're all friends here," said Uncle Alec, holding up his hands placatingly. "And Odelia only writes her stories after checking them with me first."

"That still doesn't explain how she could possibly know about this case already," he insisted.

"A little birdie told me, all right? Now can you or can't you confirm that Paulo Frey's body was found at the bottom of the Writer's Lodge outhouse?"

"Yes, I can," said the Chief, casting a weary glance at the new detective.

"Unbelievable," huffed Kingsley again, shaking his head.

She turned on the man. "This is the way we do things in this town."

"It's certainly different from the way we handle things in the city," he said, giving her a very stern look. "In fact I can't even imagine any nosy reporter ever barging into the office of the NYPD commissioner and dictating terms."

"I'm not dictating terms," she said. "I'm merely trying to get confirmation on some basic facts pertaining to this case."

"A case you have no business sticking your nose into."

"It *is* my business because I choose to *make* it my business."

"Oh? Last time I checked you weren't on the police payroll, Miss Poole."

"Odelia is part of the family, Chase," said Uncle Alec, finally managing to get a word in edgewise. "We're all on the same page here. One great team."

The detective held up his hands. "All right, Chief. But I still think it's extremely unorthodox, and if I were you I'd reconsider the leeway you're granting your niece."

"Well, you're not me, son," said the Chief with a smile.

"Yes, Detective Kingsley, you're not the chief of police in

this town," said Odelia. "So please stop sticking your nose where it doesn't belong."

Perhaps she shouldn't have said that, for the man's eyes narrowed dangerously. In fact they now reminded her of twin laser beams, doing their utmost to blast through her skull and incinerate her on the spot. She swallowed. She had the impression it probably wasn't wise to be on his bad side.

Uncle Alec cleared his throat noisily. "So, about Paulo Frey. I can confirm that we found his body at the bottom of the Writer's Lodge outhouse well and that it's been trans-ferred to the coroner's office for an autopsy."

"Do you think he fell down that well by accident?"

"Considering the fact that his luggage, his clothes, his laptop and all of his other belongings were also down there, I think it's safe to say he was murdered. But like I said, it's all up to the medical examiner now to know for sure."

"Do you have any leads on the killer?"

"None yet."

"When did he disappear again? I seem to remember sometime last year?"

"It's been over a year," the Chief confirmed, then shook his head. "It's going to be very hard to figure out what exactly happened."

She thought she understood. After such a long time there probably wasn't much left of the famous writer. "Did you..." She swallowed. "Did you see the body?"

He nodded, a grim set to his face. "Yes, I did. We had to disassemble the outhouse and get the cesspool pumping guys in there. Took us the better part of yesterday. The body was pretty decomposed when we finally found it at the bottom. Practically all that's left is a skeleton with some remnants of skin and hair." He sighed. "Not a pretty sight, Odelia."

"So how do you know it's Paulo Frey?"

"Well, we found his ID, laptop, smartphone, luggage...

Hard to tell from the body, of course. But I'm pretty sure dental records will back us up."

"And DNA."

"Yeah, if necessary they'll do a DNA test, I'm sure. But I think dental will provide adequate proof of identity, and much quicker, too."

"Darn it, Uncle Alec. An actual murder in Hampton Cove."

"It's a nasty business," he agreed. "A very nasty business indeed."

"You don't get a lot of murders down here?" asked Detective Kingsley.

"None," said Odelia and her uncle simultaneously.

"This is a very peaceful town, Detective Kingsley," said Odelia. "In fact I wonder what a big-city cop like you is doing down here."

"I have my reasons," he said.

"Let's just say that Chase here needed a change of pace," said the Chief pacifically. "And we're mighty glad he chose Hampton Cove. The NYPD's loss is definitely our gain," he stressed, giving Odelia a keen look. "We need men like Chase on the force. None of us are getting any younger."

Oh, shoot. Was Uncle Alec thinking about retiring and appointing Chase Kingsley as his replacement? Then she'd just antagonized the next chief of police!

She nodded, and a look of understanding passed between herself and her uncle. She would cut the new detective some slack. But then she remembered something else, and turned to the detective again. "Could you please do something about that cat of yours, Detective Kingsley?"

His eyebrows shot up. "My... cat?"

"Yes. He's been throwing his weight around all over town, scaring the local cats and behaving as if he owns the place.

More specifically, he's been terrorizing my own cat Max. Really behaving like a bully, you know."

Detective Kingsley's eyebrows shot up even further into his fringe. "Your cat Max."

She nodded seriously. "He actually chased him out of the park last night…" She was going to add that he'd also barred Max access to the police station, but stopped herself.

Her uncle coughed. "Odelia loves her cat, don't you, honey?"

Detective Kingsley barked an incredulous laugh. "I don't believe this. You're telling me that *my* cat is bullying *your* cat?"

She pursed her lips. "That's exactly what I'm saying. You can't simply barge into town and start throwing your weight around, Detective."

He rolled his eyes. "I'll keep it in mind."

"So you better have a chat with your cat and tell him to behave, all right?"

The detective threw up his hands. "Oh, sure! Absolutely! I'll have a 'chat' with my cat. Is there anything else you would like me to do, Miss Poole? Tell the begonias not to take up so much space in the garden? Cause God knows they shouldn't simply barge in here and start bullying other plants in other gardens!"

"You're making fun of me, aren't you?"

"No, *you're* making fun of *me!*" he snapped, then turned away from her, muttering something under his breath that didn't sound very nice.

"Well, that's settled then," said the Chief, placing his hands on his desk. He was looking uncomfortable. "Chase will have a word with his cat, and—"

"—as soon as you hear from the coroner's office—"

"—I'll be sure to give you a call," he finished with a wide smile.

33

"Of course you will," Detective Kingsley added with another eye roll.

She turned. "You'll soon find that down here in Hampton Cove we do things differently than in the big city, Detective," she snapped.

"You don't say," he muttered.

"So I suggest you get used to it," she added, and without deigning him another glance, swept from the office and slammed the door behind her.

CHAPTER 5

I decided to return to the house and regroup. This whole business with Brutus had thrown me for a loop. If you can't even go where you want in your own town, it's a sad state of affairs. So when I arrived in my own backyard again, I felt both relieved—this was most definitely my personal domain and no domineering cat could tell me otherwise—and annoyed, for I suddenly felt cooped up for the first time in my life. When you're a free spirit and suddenly you're forcibly confined to your own backyard, it's not much fun.

I suddenly felt what prisoners must feel like once they find themselves locked up in the pokey. I even had the orange jumpsuit to go with my current position. Well, not the jumpsuit, maybe. But definitely the appropriate color.

The moment I set foot in my yard, Harriet and Dooley came trotting up. They appear to have a sixth sense about these things. Or maybe they simply gab a lot. Word spreads fast in our small Hampton Cove cat community.

"What happened?" asked Harriet. She seemed genuinely worried, which felt like balm to my wounded pride.

"Yeah, what's going on?" Dooley asked. "I heard you got kicked out of the police station by that brute Brutus?"

"And is it true that a man was murdered?" asked Harriet, eyes wide.

"How do you guys even know about that already?"

"Well, Stacy Brown's cat witnessed the standoff between you and Brutus, and Father Reilly's tabby Shanille was out snooping around the Writer's Lodge yesterday," said Harriet, studying her paw intently. "The place was crawling with police, and next thing she knew an ambulance rode up and took away what looked like a cadaver. She had to move upwind at some point, as the place was reeking to high heaven." She wrinkled her nose. "Shanille said they found the body in the lodge's poo-poo pit."

"It's true," I confirmed. "They found the body of that writer that went missing last year. Paulo Frey, remember? He used to stay at the lodge at least once a year, to write his best-sellers, and last year he vanished without a trace."

"So they found him?" asked Dooley, giving his tush a swift lick. All this talk about poo seemed to have inspired him. What can I say? We cats are a very suggestible bunch.

"So what happened? Did he commit suicide? Jump into the pit?" asked Harriet, her green eyes glittering with excitement. "Why would he do that?"

"Humans love poo," said Dooley sagely. "So this man must have wanted to take a bath in the stuff and accidentally drowned. It's the latest craze."

I stared at him. "What are you talking about?"

"It's true. Out in Hollywood they take baths in their own poo now. It's supposed to rejuvenate the skin and get rid of wrinkles. And that's not the only thing. They even drink their own pee," he added knowingly. "First thing in the morning. It's like a tonic. They call it the juice of life."

"That's crazy," I said. "Nobody takes a bath in their own

poo, except perhaps pigs, but that's because they don't know any better."

"No, I'm telling you, Max. It's a real thing," said Dooley. "Celebrities smear their own poo on their faces all the time. It's even been on that website POOP."

"GOOP," Harriet corrected. "Not POOP."

Gwyneth Paltrow's website was a hit with Hampton Covians as she was a local girl made good. I never met her, as she spends most of her time in Amagansett, but I'm a fan, and so are all the other cats. Her site often features articles on what cats are thinking. It's all very droll and entertaining.

"I'm pretty sure Miss Paltrow would never propagate something silly like smearing poo on your face," I said, though maybe she would. The things that celebrities do to try and stay young are fascinating and frankly amazing.

"It's a thing," Dooley insisted stubbornly.

"Anyway," I said, trying to get the conversation back on track. "Paulo Frey didn't take a bath in his own poo. He was killed and then his body was dumped in there so nobody would find out. At least that's what the police think. Since they also found his laptop in there, and all of his belongings." I cocked an eye at Dooley. "If he wanted to take a bath, would he have jumped in with his laptop?"

Dooley shrugged. "Maybe he wanted to take notes while he was taking a bath? Writers are funny people, Max. Or maybe he was researching the perfect murder, decided to try out this poo thing for himself and got in way over his head."

Harriet laughed. "Funny, Dooley. Way over his head."

Dooley gave her a blank stare. He didn't get the joke.

Dooley was right, though. Writers are a little eccentric. Year after year they come to the Writer's Lodge to hatch up their harebrained plots, roaming the woods muttering to themselves, or soaking in the Jacuzzi Hetta has installed for their benefit, staring up at the sky and begging the gods of creativity to help them out when they get stuck. But even though they might be eccentric, they're not so eccentric they'd jump into an outhouse with all of their personal belongings and their laptop. No, this case had the stench of foul play all over it.

"He was killed," I said adamantly. "Uncle Alec is sure of it. Now all he needs is cause and time of death, which the medical examiner will hopefully figure out from what's left of the body, and then he can start his investigation."

"Who's running the investigation?" asked Harriet. "Is it true that Uncle Alec is handing it to Mr. Dreamboat?"

"How do you even know about that?" I asked. I was starting to wonder if all my snooping around the police office was even necessary. If Harriet could find out as much as I had simply by talking to other cats, what was the point?

"It's only common sense," she said. "Chase Kingsley used to be a NYPD detective, after all, so what better person to run a murder investigation than him, correct?"

"It's so cool, right?" said Dooley. "An actual NYPD detective investigating an actual murder in our town."

"Way cool," Harriet agreed with a smile.

"If he's so cool, what is he doing here?" I asked. "Why didn't he stay in New York?" It was a question that begged asking. If this hotshot detective was so great, why choose to bury himself in a small town like Hampton Cove, where the homicide rate was probably close to zero?

Harriet stared at me. "Don't you know?"

"Know what?"

"Well, he was fired."

"Fired! But why?" Now this was news. If I'd known this before, I could have told Odelia. Make sure she didn't do something silly like fall in love with the man.

Harriet slowly and methodically started licking her paw and then rubbing it across her face. "Gross misconduct. At least that's what Shanille said, who heard it from Buster, Fido Siniawski's cat, who read it in the *New York Post.*"

"That's impossible," I scoffed. "If Chase Kingsley was fired for gross misconduct, he would never be able to work as a police officer again, not even in Hampton Cove. No," I mused, "it must be something else."

"Shanille was pretty adamant. And you know that tabloids never lie."

"Right. They wouldn't dare," I said. Could it be? Could Detective Kingsley have been a bad boy? Why else would he accept a job here? Not for the excitement. Unless riding around in a dune buggy was his idea of excitement.

"What's gross misconduct?" asked Dooley. "Is it really gross, Max?"

"It's something to do with the wife of a suspect," said Harriet. "She claims Detective Kingsley molested her during an interrogation, so she filed charges against him. He was consequently suspended pending a full investigation, and eventually forced to hand in his gun and his badge, his employment effectively terminated."

I stared at her. "He was discharged for molesting the wife of a suspect and you still think he's a dreamboat?"

"I don't believe it, all right?" she said, holding up her paw, then continuing to groom the left side of her face. "I'm sure that poor man was framed."

"Framed?" I asked, incredulous.

"It happens all the time, Max. Detective Kingsley got framed. At least that's what Brutus says and I believe him."

"Brutus says his human was framed," I said blankly. Now I'd heard it all.

"Brutus said he saw something he wasn't supposed to see, and so they set him up to destroy his credibility. It happens all the time," she added when she caught my dubious look. "Successful people get a lot of flak. And I'm sure this woman who accused him must have perjured herself."

"That must have hurt," said Dooley.

"Perjured, Dooley," I said automatically. "Not injured."

I was thinking hard. This changed matters entirely. If this was true, and I didn't doubt it since Brutus himself had confirmed the story, Odelia had to be warned. I was sure that once she found out who Chase Kingsley really was, that she would never want to come anywhere near the man. Which would take care of the Brutus emergency nicely.

"I'm telling Odelia," I said therefore. "She needs to know who she's dealing with."

Harriet sighed. "I was afraid of this. Can't you just let it go, Max?"

"Let it go!"

"Why can't you just give Odelia a shot at real happiness? I'm sure that she and Chase are simply made for each other. Two beautiful people like that? It's a match made in heaven. The moment they walk down the aisle together, we'll all be family." She sighed again, wistfully this time. "You, me, Dooley… Brutus… just one big happy family."

"One big happy family with Brutus? I don't think so," I said. "That cat kicked me out of the police station, Harriet! Actually forbade me to even go there. How can I do my job if I can't even eavesdrop on Odelia's uncle?"

"He was only doing his duty," said Harriet stiffishly. It was obvious that nothing could convince her that Brutus, and by extension Chase Kingsley, were in fact bad news.

"You can't still *like* that cat," I said, appalled. "He threatened me with violence, Harriet. Actual violence!"

Which, now that I knew what kind of person his human was, wasn't all that surprising.

"That wasn't very nice of him, was it?" Dooley said with a tentative look at Harriet.

But Harriet wasn't convinced. "I'm sure that Brutus simply feels that he's doing his duty, Max. If only more cats were like him, the world would be a better, safer place."

"The world would be one big prison camp and Brutus would run it," I said, shaking my head. I simply couldn't understand how she could still defend the cat. He was a menace to our community. "I think we should all get together and take a vote," I said now. "Have Brutus expelled. We simply cannot allow him to come here and try to take over. A red line has been crossed."

"You're simply jealous," Harriet challenged.

"Jealous!" I cried. "All I'm doing is protecting my human from a terrible fate. Is that so wrong?"

"You're absolutely right, Max," said Dooley, who was still casting anxious glances at Harriet. But then Dooley has always carried a torch for Harriet. His timid attempts at wooing her have always failed, though. Harriet doesn't like just any cat. It takes a special cat to touch her heart, and apparently in Brutus she'd found just such a cat.

A horrible thought entered my mind. "You're not thinking of getting together with Brutus, are you?" I asked, horrified.

She gave me a dark look. "Please, Max, don't be silly."

"I think we should continue this investigation ourselves," I now said, deciding to change the subject. "If it's true that Chase was dishonorably discharged from the NYPD, I can't imagine he's fit to lead the investigation into this murder."

"So we do it ourselves?" asked Dooley excitedly.

"We do it ourselves," I confirmed. "We catch that killer."

"I don't know, Max," said Harriet dubiously. "Do you think we're up for it? I mean, we've never done anything like this before. It might be dangerous."

"We owe it to Hampton Cove to catch any killer that might be lurking in our community," I said solemnly. "And we need to make sure that the Writer's Lodge is once again safe for writers to scribble their creative scribblings."

"I hadn't thought about that," said Harriet pensively.

"Do you think writers are going to avoid the Writer's Lodge as long as the killer isn't caught?" asked Dooley.

"I'm sure no writer wants to take up residence at a lodge where only recently one of their kind has been gruesomely murdered. At least not as long as the killer is still lurking out in those woods, looking for their next potential victim."

"Stephen King might like it," Dooley said. "It might give him inspiration for another one of his horror stories."

"Yes," I amended, "Stephen King might like it."

"Or George R. R. Martin," Harriet said. "He'd probably love the idea of a writer being murdered at a writer's lodge."

"Yes, Mr. Martin might get a kick out of it," I agreed.

"And what about J.K. Rowling?" asked Dooley. "She loves a good horror story. Ooh! Maybe Voldemort returned from the dead and killed Paulo Frey!"

"Somehow I doubt it, Dooley," I said. "Okay, so I'm prepared to concede that there are certain writers who wouldn't mind staying at a lodge where a fellow writer was brutally murdered, but apart from them I'm sure most writers will think twice before selecting the Writer's Lodge as a destination for their next writer's retreat. Which means Hetta Fried stands to lose her livelihood, and Hampton Cove a time-honored tradition of hosting famous celebrity writers in our midst."

"And the liquor store a great deal of business," Dooley added.

He was right. A lot of writers enjoyed raiding the liquor store before starting a new book. Apparently copious amounts of alcohol are a surefire way to tackle writer's block.

"In conclusion," I said, "I feel that it is our sacred duty as proud residents of Hampton Cove to find out who killed Mr. Paulo Frey and to bring them to justice."

"I agree. Let's find ourselves a killer," Harriet said, momentarily halting her grooming efforts—it takes a lot of effort to keep that snowy white fur looking perfectly fluffy and immaculately clean. She held up her paw.

I placed my own blorange paw against hers, and Dooley raised his.

"We solemnly swear to catch a killer and bring them to justice," we intoned, and then let go, satisfied we'd made a momentous pledge.

"So when do we start?" asked Dooley.

"Tonight," I said, yawning. I needed my beauty sleep. It had been too long since I had enjoyed a nice nap.

"Good idea," Harriet agreed. "Let's take a long nap and meet up tonight."

And showing she wasn't joking, she immediately trotted off in the direction of her own backyard, stared after by Dooley and me.

"Um, can I sleep on your couch, Max?" asked Dooley.

"Why? Don't you have enough space at your place?"

Dooley gave me a hesitant look. "It's not that. It's just that…"

"What is it? Did Harriet take all the best spots again?"

He nodded sheepishly. That's the trouble when you live in the same house as a Persian. They like to think they are the lord of the manor. Queen of the castle. Ruler of the realm. Reducing all others to playing second fiddle.

"Of course," I said. "You can sleep on my couch. Now let's get our eighteen hours in before we go and catch ourselves a killer."

CHAPTER 6

The moment Odelia returned to the newspaper, she drew up a list of people to interview. She wanted not just to solve this murder, but to write a series of articles that would have Hampton Covians sticking to their newspaper like glue, reading with rapt attention as their intrepid reporter led them, clue by clue, to the revelation of the identity of the killer who'd murdered one of their own. Well, technically Paulo Frey wasn't one of their own, of course. He was a New Yorker who spent a couple of weeks a year out there. But still, since Hampton Cove was a tourist town, tourists were as much a part of the community as the locals who lived there year-round.

Besides, even in the heart of winter tourists stayed in town, as the tourist board had added a couple of winter events to the schedule, in the hope of making the town more attractive when the weather turned inclement.

They organized a Winterfest, and a Christmas market with an ice rink. It worked, for even in winter tourists made their way out there, though of course not as many as in the summer months, when the beaches were full of people cavorting in the surf and enjoying all-night parties.

The only one who didn't care for the new winter activities was Uncle Alec, who now had to round up drunk revelers all year, and not just during the summer.

"So? Got yourself a genuine murder case?" Dan asked, leaning against the doorjamb. He was sipping from his umpteenth cup of coffee and looked excited, as excited as she was feeling herself. He was a shortish man in his late sixties, with an impressive white beard and plenty of laugh wrinkles around his eyes, which always seemed to twinkle with delight.

"Yup. This is the big one, Dan. Famous bestselling writer gets murdered and dumped in the last Long Island outhouse. This is going to get national headlines, I'm sure."

"Do they have a suspect?" asked the veteran editor.

"Not yet. Uncle Alec put Chase Kingsley in charge."

This caused the editor's bushy brows to wiggle with surprise. "Chase Kingsley? The new detective?"

"Yeah, he's supposed to be this hotshot detective from New York. Apparently he used to work for the NYPD, so he's well qualified."

"*Used* to work being the operative word."

She stared at him. "What do you mean?"

All she knew about the guy was that he had an annoying cat, and that he seemed to hate reporters. Or it could be that he just hated her, of course.

Dan looked over his shoulder, as if fully expecting Detective Kingsley to walk into the office to eavesdrop on their private conversation.

"What I've heard is that Chase Kingsley didn't quit the NYPD but was forced out." He lowered his brows and grumbled in a low voice, "Fired for gross misconduct is what I heard. Molestation of a suspect's wife."

"Molestation!" she cried, her jaw dropping. "No way!"

He shook his head sadly. "All I know is what was printed in the *New York Post*."

"Oh, my" she said, reaching for her laptop. This she had to see.

"It was actually Fido Siniawski who remembered reading something about a rogue detective a couple of months ago. So he told me and I looked it up and he was right. I doubt your uncle knows about this, otherwise he probably would never have hired the man." His voice took on a grave tone. "If the rumors are true he molested the wife of a suspect while the guy was in custody, and she pressed charges against him, apparently not too keen on being manhandled by a cop."

She stared at the editor, aghast. "You're kidding me."

Dan shrugged. "Do I look like I'm kidding?"

"But why would Uncle Alec hire a guy like that?"

"Like I said, he probably doesn't know."

"That's impossible. Nobody hires an officer from another department without checking their credentials first."

"Maybe Detective Kingsley lied on his resume?"

"I find it hard to believe Uncle Alec wouldn't check his references. The NYPD is only a phone call away. No, I'm sure he knows about Kingsley's past and simply chose to ignore it." She frowned. "But why?"

"Beats me. I just know that that uncle of yours has got a really big heart, Odelia. Maybe he felt sorry for the guy? Heck, I'm not saying he's not a good cop. Everyone seems to agree he's one hell of a detective. But with a thing like that hanging over his head, his chances of ever working as a police officer again were probably slim to nonexistent."

"Except down here in Hampton Cove." If she hadn't been furious with the detective before, she was furious now. Molestation charges were not something to be taken lightly.

"Except in Hampton Cove," Dan agreed with a nod.

"I have to talk to Uncle Alec about this. We can't have a man like that working for the HCPD. Especially with the whole town knowing about his sordid past. How can he expect to assume a position of authority?"

"We don't know if the allegations are true. For all we know the charges were unfounded and he was forced out."

"I don't think the NYPD would let him go if the charges were unfounded," she argued. "No, this is serious stuff, Dan. If this is true, we can't have a man like that working in our town."

"You better have that talk with your uncle. Thresh this thing out once and for all." He grinned at her. "So looks like you've got yourself two stories to dig into, mh? A murder and a bad cop. This is your lucky day."

CHAPTER 7

Ten minutes later, she waltzed into her dad's doctor's office again, and walked straight up to the desk. Gran, who'd been playing Scrabble online, eyed her disapprovingly. She didn't like being interrupted when she was on a winning streak. "I told you. I'm fine. It was just a stomach bug. I'm all right now."

"Good to know," she said, panting slightly. "Is Rohanna still here?"

Gran raised her eyebrows, then gestured with her head to one of the examination rooms. "In there. What do you want with her?"

Odelia dropped her voice to a whisper. "There's been a murder, and I'm writing the story. Remember that writer who disappeared last year?"

"That nutcase?" asked Gran, making no effort to lower her voice.

"Yeah, that nutcase," she whispered. "Well, he didn't disappear. He was murdered. They just dredged up his body from the Writer's Lodge outhouse."

"You don't say," said Gran, licking her lips with obvious glee. "And you think Rohanna did it?"

"No, I don't. But I remember she also works for Hetta, cleaning the Writer's Lodge. So I just figured she might be a good place to start my investigation. Maybe she saw something or remembers something."

"I doubt it," said Gran. "The woman is loony."

"Why do you think she's loony?" she asked after a pause. Gran sometimes had a habit of judging people too harshly, and being very vocal about it.

"Because she keeps singing to herself, that's why. I caught her at it a couple of times." She leaned closer, but still spoke loud enough so that everyone in the waiting room could hear her. "She sings to herself and wiggles that enormous tush of hers while she works. Can you believe it?"

Odelia smiled. "Plenty of people sing while they work, Gran."

"Well, I don't."

"That's because you have to answer the phone, and talk to people. Rohanna listens to music and sings along just to make the work go faster."

"I'm telling you, the woman is loony. Either you work, or you shake your ass. You can't do both, unless you're an exotic dancer, and trust me, no one is going to pay good money to watch Rohanna Coral strip and hug a pole."

"Gran!"

"What? It's true."

Shaking her head, Odelia went in search of Rohanna. She checked examination room number two, which served as a backup in case Dad's workload became too much, and he called in the assistance of a colleague. She found Rohanna, earbuds in her ears, softly humming along with the music, shaking her tush, just like Gran said.

She was a large woman, and had a considerable tush to shake, that was true enough, though Odelia didn't see anything wrong with a person enjoying their job. She tried to catch Rohanna's attention, and finally walked up to her and gave her a tap on the shoulder. Rohanna removed the earbuds and eyed her askance, as if to say, 'What do you want?'

"Hey, Rohanna," she said. "Sorry to bother you, but could I ask you a couple of questions about Paulo Frey and the Writer's Lodge?"

If the name was familiar to the cleaning lady, she didn't give any indication. Instead, she frowned and asked, "Who?"

"Paulo Frey? He was one of the writers who used to stay at the Writer's Lodge. One of the regulars. He disappeared last year."

Her frown deepened. It was obvious she didn't like being interrupted while she was working. Or perhaps her favorite song had been on, and she hated to miss the opportunity to sing along. "I think I remember him," she finally said. "Isn't he the skinny one who writes those gruesome thrillers?"

"He was a thriller writer," she confirmed. Whether he was skinny was up for debate. Judging from the pictures she'd googled he looked pretty average.

"What about him? Did he finally decide to show up again?"

"Well, he did show up," she said, wondering how to break the news gently. "Um, Rohanna, you might want to sit down for this." She gestured at one of the chairs and Rohanna, shaking her head and clearly not happy about this interruption of her routine, still did as she was told.

"Are you gonna tell me what's going on?" she asked.

In a few carefully chosen words she explained that the police had fished the body of Paulo Frey out of the cesspit, and Rohanna was understandably shaken. She placed a hand on her voluminous chest, which was heaving. "Dead?" she asked, a quiver in her voice. "He's dead? But how?"

"He was murdered, Rohanna," Odelia said gently. "Someone murdered him and tried to hide the body."

"Oh, my God," said the cleaner, her face a mask of distress. "He was such a nice man. A great tipper. Always left me a big tip at the end of his stay. Said I was the best, on account of the fact that I always left a bottle of bourbon on the nightstand when he arrived. Hetta wants me to leave chocolates, and I usually do, but Paulo told me the first year he hated chocolate. So I always left him one of those small bottles of bourbon."

"I see," she said. "So he was fond of the drink?"

But Rohanna wasn't listening. She shook her head. "He was always full of stories and jokes. A real live wire. Whenever I was down at the lodge he used to tell me stories of his writing career. The most hilarious stuff. He once told me he had dinner with the President and the First Lady at the White House, and he and the President got drunk and decided to play golf on the White House lawn. In the middle of the night!" She looked up at Odelia. "Who did it, Miss Poole? You tell me who did this and I'll kill the bastard."

"They don't know yet. The police only found the body yesterday."

"How?"

Odelia explained about the laptop, and Rohanna nodded. "He was crazy about that laptop. He had all of his manuscripts on that thing. All of his precious books. His entire life's work. He never went anywhere without that laptop. It would have been impossible for that laptop to be down there and not Paulo himself…" She swallowed with difficulty, tears suddenly flooding her eyes, and broke off.

"It's all right, Rohanna," Odelia said, dragging a few paper tissues from a dispenser on her father's desk and handing them to the woman. As soon as she'd wiped her eyes, she gently asked, "I want you to think hard. Do you know if Paulo had any enemies? Anyone who would want to harm him?"

Rohanna shook her head in dismay, then finally choked out, "All I remember is that one day he told me about his feud with Aissa Spring."

"Aissa Spring of No Spring Chicks?"

"That's the one. He used to go there for dinner sometimes. Until he discovered that Aissa's partner…" She raised her eyes to meet Odelia's. "That she's big."

She frowned. Aissa Spring lived with her girlfriend Marissa Dixon. Together they ran a vegetarian restaurant in town.

"Big? What do you mean, big?"

"Well, Marissa is a big girl, and apparently Paulo had a thing against big girls."

"I don't understand."

"You better ask Aissa about it," said Rohanna, loudly blowing her nose. "Apparently Paulo insulted Marissa when he was there, and Aissa kicked him out. I just thought it was a little weird for a write of his stature to have this hang-up."

Yes, that was a little weird. She now realized she didn't know all that much about Paulo Frey. Apart from the fact that he was a million-selling writer of thrillers, the guy was a mystery to her.

"Thanks, Rohanna. I'll go and have a word with Aissa."

"You do that, and nail the person that did this."

Before she left the room, she turned and said, "Oh, the police will probably want to have a word with you as well."

Rohanna nodded. "I'll tell them exactly the same thing I told you."

"It won't be my uncle, though. Chase Kingsley is in charge of the investigation."

Rohanna's eyes lit up. "Chase Kingsley? Oh, he's fine."

Odelia grimaced. "If you say so."

"Oh, he can interrogate me anytime," said Rohanna, her distress over Paulo Frey's murder quickly making way for a different emotion altogether.

She managed to give Rohanna a grimace at this, thinking hard thoughts about the detective. She needed to get to the bottom of that story, too, and as soon as she revealed that Kingsley was a notorious molester of women, she was pretty sure people like Rohanna would think differently of him.

But first things first. She needed to talk to Aissa Spring. She was the first person who might have a motive for murder. And she was just passing through the corridor on her way to the waiting room, when she bumped into her dad, emerging from the examination room with a patient in tow.

"Oh, hey, honey," he said, giving her a quick peck on the cheek. "If you came to check up on your grandmother, she's fine. I tried to give her a checkup this morning and she brushed me off, insisting she was in better shape than me."

"Yeah, I know," she said with a smile. "She's probably in better shape than all of us."

Her father was a big bluff man, well-liked by his patients. He had a knack for putting anyone at ease in a matter of seconds, and often only needed a glance to know what was ailing his patients. They were two qualities that explained his popularity as Hampton Cove's premier family doctor.

"See you tonight?" he asked now.

"Yes, Dad," she said, briefly wondering whether to tell him about the murder but quickly deciding against it. They could discuss it over dinner.

"Your mother invited a guest," he said as he waved the next patient in.

"A guest?" she asked. "You mean Uncle Alec?"

"Yeah, Alec is coming, and he's bringing one of his

colleagues," her father said as he walked into his office. Before he closed the door, he frowned. "What was his name again…" Then his face cleared. "Oh, that's right. Chase Kingsley. A new cop. See you later, honey." And then he closed the door and she was left staring at it, a look of abject horror written all over her features.

CHAPTER 8

J was still feeling a little groggy and unsteady on my paws. Usually I like to take my eighteen hours of sleep in one long stretch, interspersed with the occasional run to the litter box and the feeding trough. Today, though, I was a cat on a mission, so I'd decided to cut my nap time short and head downtown to see what I could find out about the case of the murdered writer.

I never follow a strict plan on these trips of mine but simply go where my paws take me. I have my regular haunts, of course. Places where I can find the best information. Like the barbershop, the doctor's office, or the police station. For some strange reason I always happen to be in the right place at the right time. Call it cat's intuition. It's a very powerful thing, let me tell you. And I'd just wandered out into the street, when Dooley fell into step beside me, looking even more haggard than I was feeling.

"Couldn't sleep, Max?" he asked as we trundled along the sidewalk.

"Duty calls, Dooley," I said a little solemnly. "You simply can't wait around for the next clue to arrive on its own. A genuine detective goes out there, into the great unknown, and hunts the clues where he can find them."

Dooley yawned. "I couldn't sleep either. All this stuff about Brutus and that gruesome poo murder had me wondering about my mortality."

I stared at my friend. I never would have guessed that Dooley even knew the word 'mortality' let alone pondered about his own perishability. In fact I'd never known him to worry about anything, except when Marge, Odelia's mom, dished out the wrong kibble. Dooley likes chicken, but Marge tends to forget, and buys him those twenty-pound bags of fish kibble which he then has to eat, because she hates to throw away perfectly good kibble. What can I say? We all have our predilections and peculiarities.

"Do you really think Brutus is going to move in with us and lay down the law, Max?" he now asked.

"I think the odds are not in our favor," I confirmed. "Chase Kingsley is a very handsome male human, and Odelia is an attractive female. What's more, they're both young and single, and live in a town with a limited supply of eligible bachelors. And if I know something about human nature, it's that eligible bachelors are prone to mate, and when they do, they tend to make babies and get married and move in together, at which point they bring their cats along."

Dooley shook his head sadly. It was obvious he wasn't liking this. "I didn't want to say this in front of Harriet, because she seems to like this Brutus so very much, but I honestly fear for our lives when Brutus moves in, Max."

I looked up in surprise. "Fear for our lives? What do you mean?"

"Well, Brutus strikes me as the kind of cat who doesn't like competition in the home. I'm pretty sure that once he moves in he's going to want to make us disappear so he will be the only cat in the house. If you know what I mean."

"You're saying he's gonna want to kill us?"

"You, me, and maybe even Harriet when she doesn't do what he says. Cats like that want to be the supreme rulers, Max. They're like the evil stepchild who tries to kill their stepsiblings once they've taken up position in the home."

"You mean like Damien in *The Omen*?" I asked, remembering the horror movie marathon Odelia had us sit through the other night. Harriet, Dooley and I had been scared stiff the entire time, but Odelia had loved the story of Satan's spawn. She loves a good horror movie, while the three of us prefer to watch *Garfield*. Or *Finding Nemo*. I never get tired of watching those fishes in that fish tank. *Finding Dory* was even better. Much bigger tank.

"Well, maybe more like *The Good Son*," said Dooley after a moment's deliberation. After a lifetime spent with Odelia, he knows his horror classics even better than me.

"I don't think Brutus is going to kill us," I said thoughtfully.

"And I'm sure he is. He's going to strike when we're all sleeping safely in our beds."

I shivered. Maybe Dooley was right. Clearly this Brutus was capable of anything. Now, more than ever, I was convinced we needed to figure out a way to make Odelia see what kind of a man Chase Kingsley really was. If we could convince her he was a genuine menace, we could avert the Brutus disaster.

And it was as we were crossing the street, wondering where to go next, that I saw Chase enter the doctor's office. I nudged Dooley. "Speak of the devil. It's him!"

"Great!" said Dooley, his dejected air quickly giving way to excitement. "Do you think we'll find some more damaging information about the guy?"

"One can only hope," I said, and we quickly made our way down the narrow alleyway that divides the doctor's office from Jeremiah Downer's hardware store. We hopped over a pile of plastic trash bags, and then onto a couple of trash cans, a dumpster and straight onto the windowsill of Tex's consulting room. I felt pumped. Now we were going to find out what really made Detective Kingsley tick. In all my years in Hampton Cove I'd never been able to glean more about the local populace than by eavesdropping on the good Dr. Poole while he was chatting with his patients.

You'd be surprised what people tell their doctor, knowing he's not allowed to divulge their secrets to another living soul, due to something called the doctor-patient privilege. Good thing those silly rules don't apply to cats!

Dooley and I both peered into the window, and saw that Chase had already been led into the consulting room and had taken a seat across from Odelia's father. He was lucky to arrive when there were no other patients present.

"My dear young man," Tex said as he took a seat and smiled at his new patient. "Tell me, what can I do for you?"

"Well, you probably don't know me, Doc," Chase said.

"Nonsense," said Tex. "You're that new police detective, aren't you? The one my brother-in-law speaks so highly of. Detective Chase Kingsley?"

Chase seemed surprised, though he shouldn't have been. Nothing remained a secret very long in Hampton Cove. And definitely not the arrival of a new cop in town.

He eyed the doctor a little wearily. "Um... What else did Alec tell you?"

"Oh, that you are a most valuable addition to our police force, that's all," said Tex amiably as he leaned back and folded his hands behind his head. "We can definitely use a good man like you, Detective. There might not be a lot of crime in this town, but tourism is increasing by leaps and bounds, and trust me when I tell you that those whipper-snappers are capable of a lot of mischief."

"Yeah, Alec told me," said Chase with a grimace. He leaned forward and appeared a little flustered. "Listen, Doc, um, the reason I'm here is because, well, I need a new prescription since I'm all out of meds." At this, he placed a piece of paper on the desk between the two men.

"And what prescription would that be?" Tex asked, snapping up the piece of paper and placing a pair of glasses on his nose to give it a closer look.

I pricked up my ears and so did Dooley. I was pretty sure we were on the verge of discovering yet another damning secret about Chase Kingsley. One that would permanently turn Odelia against him.

Tex was still frowning at the slip of paper, then placed it on his blotter. "You having trouble sleeping, son?"

"Amongst other things," Chase admitted. "My New York doctor gave me those to take the edge off and to help me sleep. I…" He hesitated.

"Anxiety attacks can be extremely debilitating," Tex said with a nod as he placed his glasses on his desk. "Especially in your line of work, Detective."

Chase nodded morosely, then rubbed his cheek with his hands. Finally he looked up, and I saw he suddenly looked extremely tired. "I don't know if…"

"Trust me, son," said Tex with his deep, sonorous voice that had the effect of putting his patients immediately at ease. His bedside manner was impeccable. "Whatever you tell me stays between us. You have my word on that."

"That's not necessarily true," Dooley muttered next to me.

"The thing is, Doc, is that I find myself in a real quandary."

"Oh? Does it have something to do with the Mayor's wife?"

Chase seemed surprised, and so was I. The Mayor's wife?

"I see that Alec told you the story already."

"He did tell me a few things."

"Then you also know that I was set up?" asked Chase.

"I'm afraid Alec didn't go into a lot of detail. All he told me was that you ran afoul of the Mayor's wife, who launched a scandalous story about you in retaliation, which forced you out of the NYPD. He also told me that none of the rumors about you are true and that you're a decent man and a great cop."

Chase smiled. "Alec's proven a true friend these last couple of months."

"He was a friend of your father, correct?"

"Yeah. They went to police academy together. In fact Alec is my godfather, and when my dad died—killed in the line of duty—he kept dropping by the house occasionally, effectively becoming like a surrogate father. He's one of the few people who know the truth about my resignation." His lips thinned.

"If you want, you can tell me," Tex offered. "Like I said, my lips are sealed."

"Thanks, Doc. It's nice to be able to talk to someone. If I could, I'd tell the whole world what happened, but that would get me into more trouble than it's worth. The thing is…" He shuffled uncomfortably in his chair for a moment. "I had the misfortune of being in the wrong place at the wrong time. A couple of months ago I was working a very sensitive case, reporting directly to the commissioner, when I happened to barge into his office one afternoon, to discover he wasn't alone. Politely put, he was in a state of undress with the Mayor's wife. In fact they were all over each other."

Tex barked an incredulous laugh. "The Mayor's wife?"

"None other than Malka Putin herself," Chase confirmed with a rueful smile. "And she wasn't glad to see me, let me tell you that. I apologized for the intrusion, but Mrs. Putin decided she couldn't leave it at that. Even though the commissioner swore me to secrecy and I agreed, she wouldn't let it go. I explained I wasn't interested in spreading gossip about other people's personal affairs, and that as far as I was concerned she could have relations with whomever she chose, it was none of my business."

"But Mrs. Putin wasn't satisfied, I take it," said Tex.

"Nope. She was afraid I'd talk. She'd heard stories about how cops like to gab, and she was sure that pretty soon the whole town would know about her affair with the commissioner, and also her husband, of course. So she convinced the commissioner to make sure I wouldn't talk."

"And he agreed?" asked Tex, surprised.

"I'm sorry to say that he did. Worse. He convinced the wife of a suspect I had in custody to concoct some harassment story in exchange for leniency for her husband. He got off with a slap on the wrist, I got to hand in my gun and badge. He figured that if he smeared my name sufficiently nobody would listen to me if I decided to talk about his affair with the Mayor's wife. People would simply think I did it out of spite, and he was right, of course."

"But Alec believed you."

"Alec has had my back from the beginning. He's one of the few people I told the truth, and believed me. He's stood by me all this time and even tried to talk some sense into the commissioner. Told him he had no right destroying the career of one of his finest to protect the reputation of Malka Putin."

"But the commissioner's loyalty to Mrs. Putin outweighed his obligation toward one of his people. That's a horrible story, Chase. A really terrible thing."

"It's taken over my life these last couple of months. My career has gone down the drain, my colleagues are avoiding me like the plague, and my chances of ever finding a job as a cop have pretty much been destroyed. So you see why I've had trouble sleeping. My doctor in New York gave me these pills and they've done wonders."

"I see." Tex toyed with the note for a moment, then said, "You know what? I'm going to do you a favor, Chase. I'm not going to give you a prescription. Instead I'm going to start a new rumor."

"You're going to do what?" asked Chase, his jaw dropping.

Tex chuckled. "This town is one big rumor mill, son. Everyone knows everyone around here, and people make it their business to butt into other people's business all the time. It's not unheard of that something happens to you on your way home and by the time you get there your wife already knows all about it!"

Chase still stared at him. "I don't get it."

"That's because you're not a Hampton Covian. Yet. I'm going to start the rumor that you were framed in this Malka Putin business, and that you're a damn fine cop. I'm going to make it so that you'll be treated like a regular hero before I'm through, Chase. As it is, people down here don't like the mayor of New York or his wife very much anyway. Trust me, you're going to come out of this smelling like roses. This community is going to embrace you as one of their own, and you'll be able to do your job as a police officer just fine."

"Are you sure that's a good idea, Doc?"

The doctor displayed a toothy grin. "I'm going to say more. I'm going to say this is one of the best ideas I've ever had. And I'm going to add this will do you a heck of a lot more good than those pills. I'm sure before long you'll feel right at home in this community. Hampton Covians are a weird bunch. They can be hostile to outsiders, even though this is a tourist town. They don't easily take to strangers, but once they do, you'll find they're the warmest, kindest people you could ever hope to meet." He gave the other man a smile that warmed my heart, and I could hear Dooley utter a happy little sigh.

Chase nodded. "If you think this will work..."

"Leave it to me. My daughter happens to be a reporter for the *Hampton Cove Gazette* and one of the most proficient and efficient gossips this town has ever known. She takes after her grandmother that way. There's not a single rumor she's not aware of, and plenty she's instigated herself. I don't know how she does it, but she always seems to know everything about everybody and often before anybody else does. If she takes up your case, your worries are over, son."

Chase looked thoughtful. "Your daughter, she doesn't happen to be blond with green eyes, does she?"

"That's her. Have you met?"

He grimaced. "We have, and I'm afraid we got off on the wrong foot."

"Nonsense," said Tex. "No one can get off on the wrong foot with Odelia. She's sweet as a kitten. Whatever little trouble you had will go away once you've sat down for dinner together. You are still coming to dinner, right?"

"Um..."

"Excellent. My wife told me how she told her brother to invite you."

Chase rose, looking thoughtful. He appeared on the verge of saying something, but then decided against it. "Thanks, Doc. Thanks for listening."

"Of course," Tex said, clapping the other man on his broad back and leading him out. "Trust me, before long you and Odelia will get along like a house on fire."

Chase's eyes darkened at the mention of the reporter, and I had the distinct impression he wasn't as fond of her as Tex would have liked. Which was probably a good thing, as I didn't want the two of them getting together. Still, the conversation had definitely made me see Chase in a different light. The guy wasn't so bad after all. The only thing I now held against him was his bad taste in cats, but that wasn't something he could be faulted for. Humans are easily deceived, especially the ones who can't talk with us.

Dooley and I shared a look. "That changes everything, doesn't it?" I said.

"I think it does," Dooley agreed.

"Just goes to show you can't believe everything you read in the paper."

"I knew he was a good guy, Max. I just knew it."

"No, you didn't. You thought he was bad news. We all did."

"Well, it still doesn't make the prospect of Brutus coming to live with us any better," Dooley said as we hopped down from the windowsill and started padding toward the front of the building again.

"Didn't you hear the guy? He and Odelia hate each other's guts."

"Oh. Right. So is that a good thing, you think?"

"That's a great thing. It's probably one of those instant enmities."

"Instant enemas?"

I heaved a sigh. "What's with the poo fixation today?"

"Huh?"

"Enmity, not enema. It's like instant attraction but the other way around."

He still looked puzzled. "Uh-huh."

"It happens. And a good thing, too."

We walked on in silence for a few minutes, then Dooley asked, "Are you sure about those enemas, Max? It's just that Chase didn't strike me as constipated."

I sighed. "Oh, Dooley."

CHAPTER 9

*O*delia quickly made her way over to the No Spring Chicks restaurant. She walked in and immediately crossed to the kitchen, where she knew she'd find Aissa. Even though the restaurant was doing great business, and Aissa nor Marissa had to slave behind the stove anymore but now had a chef to do the heavy lifting, Aissa still liked to stick around keeping an eye on things. At this time she could usually be found experimenting with new recipes and adding those to the menu, while Marissa was holed up in the small office in the back, poring over the books. She was the money person, while Aissa was the culinary genius.

She found Aissa in the big walk-in refrigerator, instructing the delivery man where to stash the fresh produce. She looked up when Odelia entered.

"Hey, hon," she said. "If you're here for a reservation I'm sorry to say we're fully booked tonight. Though I could always squeeze you in around eleven, if you're up for a late dinner. I'd have to give you a table at the back, though."

"That's all right. I'm having dinner at my parents' place."

"Nothing beats a home-cooked meal," said Aissa blithely

as she wiped her hands on her apron and stepped out of the refrigerator. She was a stickler for detail, which was one of the reasons No Spring Chicks was such a hit.

A rail-thin woman with a black bob, she reminded Odelia of the women manning the cafeteria counter at Hampton Cove High, who'd always been ready to ladle extra gravy onto her hash browns and provide her with an extra dollop of creamy mashed potatoes.

"So what can I do for you?" asked Aissa, and then her eyes fell on the notebook Odelia was clutching in her hand. "Official business, huh?" Her eyes lit up. "You're doing another story on No Spring Chicks? That's great! Last time you did, our reservations tripled, so keep it coming, hon. Maybe give us the front page this time."

"Well, actually I'm doing a piece on the murder of Paulo Frey," she said.

The smile instantly vanished from Aissa's face as if wiped away with a squeegee. "Yeah, I heard about that. Found him stuffed down the toilet, huh?"

She grimaced. "I take it he wasn't your favorite person in the world?"

"Not really. In fact it's safe to say Marissa and I kinda hated the guy."

At least she wasn't holding back, Odelia thought. "And why was that?"

Aissa led her through the kitchen and into the restaurant, where they took a seat at a table near the window. The place was still empty, as preparations for lunch were yet to commence. "Well, I actually liked the guy at first. When I heard he took the Writer's Lodge, Marissa and I were excited. We'd both been reading him for years. I mean, he wrote some great books. Real edge-of-your-seat type of stuff."

"I know. I've read him. The guy could write a mean thriller."

"That's the perfect word to describe the man," said Aissa, cocking an eyebrow. "He had a real mean streak."

"He did?"

Aissa nodded. "It's not something I was aware of at the time, and you certainly wouldn't have known from his books, but Paulo Frey didn't like persons of size. When he first saw Marissa, he blew a gasket. Made a scene right here in the middle of the restaurant, the place full of diners. Said she was a disgrace to humankind and used a lot of derogatory names for Marissa. He said he'd never set foot in here again, and invited everyone else to follow his example and walk out as well."

"Wow."

"Yeah. It was horrible. For a moment we were afraid everyone would do as he said, but luckily nobody seemed to care that their restaurant was being run by a plus-sized woman. So when he saw that his temper tantrum was met with eye rolls and shrugs, he stomped out, vowing to destroy us both before he was through."

"Who would have thought?"

"How such a vile man could write such great books…"

"So what happened then?"

She waved her hand. "He started spreading rumors around town that our food was poisoned, and that we were the worst cooks in the world. He even called the Food Safety and Inspection people on us. Twice. Luckily we run a clean ship around here, and they didn't shut us down."

"I wonder why I never heard about this?"

"Probably because none of the locals bought his nonsense. He was trying to rile up the tourist crowd, and doing a pretty good job, for our business effectively started to slow down. Which is when we talked to your uncle."

"And he put a stop to the nonsense."

"That wonderful man drove straight up to the Writer's Lodge and told Frey that if he ever pulled a stunt like that again he'd personally drive him out of town."

"Tarred and feathered?"

"It wouldn't surprise me," laughed Aissa. "I don't know what else he said, but it did the trick. The rumors stopped, and the customers returned."

"Except Paulo Frey."

"He wouldn't have been welcome here anyway. Not after what he put us through. The man is vile. Or at least he was," she said, sobered when she remembered the reason for this interview.

"I can understand how you felt that way," said Odelia, jotting down notes.

"And I wasn't the only one either."

"What do you mean?"

"I heard later he did the same thing to Gabby Cleret."

"The actress?"

Aissa nodded. "Drove her to a nervous breakdown."

Before Odelia could get into this, suddenly a shadow loomed over them.

"Aissa Spring?" the new arrival asked. And when she looked up, Odelia couldn't help but notice that the newcomer was giving her a not-so-friendly look.

"That's me," said Aissa. "And you are?"

"Detective Chase Kingsley," the detective said, producing a shiny new badge. "Hampton Cove Police. Can I have a word? When you're finished with Miss Poole, that is." At this, he gave Odelia another of his trademark scowls.

Aissa grinned. "My sordid past is finally catching up with me, huh?"

Odelia laughed. "Don't worry, hon. Your sordid past is safe with me." She didn't know why she said that, but she suddenly felt like protecting Aissa against this overbearing policeman. As he apparently had a history of violence against female suspects, she felt she needed to stay put and make sure nothing happened. So she returned Chase's scowl and added some heat. "It's not because Aissa had a dispute with Paulo Frey that she's automatically guilty, Detective."

"Oh, I see you've decided to become a homicide detective now," he said, gritting his teeth. He was still towering over them, blocking out the sun.

She got up and went toe to toe with the man. "I'm simply doing my job," she said. But since he had at least a foot on her, she had to crane her neck, which wasn't helping. And then there was the fact that he was wearing a very powerful cologne that assaulted her senses. Only now did she become aware of his overpowering masculinity.

Why hadn't she noticed this in Uncle Alec's office? Probably because she hadn't been quite this close to him. He was staring down at her, his icy blue eyes boring into hers, his granite face implacable, his battering ram of a chin even more impressive up close and personal. Detective Kingsley was a bad man, and she owed it to Hampton Cove to expose him, but she had to admit he was also a very attractive man, and she now experienced the full effect of his presence.

"This is a murder investigation, Miss Poole," he pointed out. "And you'd be well advised not to insert yourself into my investigation. You might get hurt."

"Is that a threat, Detective Kingsley?"

"A fair warning. Murder investigations tend to get sticky."

"I'm a reporter, Detective. It's my job to report on any crime that takes place in my town. I'm sure my uncle explained all this to you."

"He did, but that doesn't necessarily mean I agree with him," he grunted.

"Well, you'd better get used to it." She would have added

he wasn't going to be in town long enough to learn all the ins and outs of the way they did things around here, but bit her tongue. The story of Detective Kingsley's wrongdoings was one she'd crack once Frey's murderer had been caught.

While this battle of wills took place, Aissa had sat motionless. Now she noisily cleared her throat. "Did you have a question for me, Detective?"

Detective Kingsley finally dragged his eyes away from Odelia's and nodded. "I did. Where were you on the night of September sixteen last year, Miss Spring?"

This surprised Odelia. "Have you determined the time of death?"

The detective's jaw worked as he studiously chose to ignore her. "I realize it's a long time ago, but try to throw your mind back. It's important. I'm sure Miss Poole told you all about the murder of Mr. Frey by now, and the fact that we need to interview anyone who's ever been at odds with the victim."

"Yes, she did," said Aissa, with a quick look at Odelia.

From her position, Odelia was standing her ground, her arms folded across her chest. Even though it was clear the detective wanted her to leave, she refused to.

"You probably heard about our little feud?" asked Aissa sheepishly.

"I did," confirmed the detective. "Chief Lip told me how you pressed charges against Paulo Frey after he threatened to close down your restaurant and made a real stink about the fact that the restaurant was being run by…"

"A woman of size?"

"That's right."

"I was just telling Odelia what a terrible ordeal the whole thing was, and how we were worried that Frey might succeed in closing us down. Luckily Chief Lip stepped into the breach and smoothed things over. After that, Frey gave

No Spring Chicks a wide berth every time he came into town."

"How did you determine the time of death?" Odelia insisted. She'd already scribbled down the date in her little notebook: September the sixteenth.

But Detective Kingsley merely stared at Aissa, who realized she still hadn't answered the cop's question. "Oh, right," she said, quickly getting up and hurrying over to the counter. She picked up a large ledger and started flipping through it until she reached the chosen date. "The sixteenth..." she muttered, letting her finger slide down the items on the page. "Oh. Of course. We hosted the Mayor's wife's birthday bash that night, so we were pretty busy."

Odelia saw that her words had quite an impact on the overbearing detective. It was as if he stood frozen. Finally, he asked huskily, "The Mayor's wife? You mean..."

"Francine. Mayor Turner's wife? She's a vegan, so she's in here all the time."

Once again, her words had a powerful effect on the policeman. His face visibly relaxed, and a small smile indicated that her words had met his approval. "The Mayor of Hampton Cove," he said, nodding. "Not the Mayor of New York."

"Oh, no," Aissa laughed. "I don't think we've ever seen Mayor Boyce Putin here, or in Hampton Cove. He's more an Amagansett kind of person. I hear he's got quite a place out there, with a private helipad for his chopper."

"Yes, he does," the detective confirmed, his lips once again a grim line.

Odelia wondered what the story with him and Mayor Putin was, and made a quick mental note to further look into the matter.

"So if I talk to Francine Turner, she'll be able to confirm

that you were here all evening on September the sixteenth?" the detective asked now.

"I'm sure she would," said Aissa. "She's one of our best customers and I like to be here when something big like that goes down." She smiled. "Especially after what happened with Frey we were afraid we might lose the restaurant, so we made sure we worked like beavers, Marissa and I."

"Marissa was also here?"

"Yes, we were both here, I'm sure of it," she said. "It was a big thing, and we brought the birthday cake in together. It was a great night. I remember telling Francine how grateful we were for her support and the Mayor's and the entire Hampton Cove community." She gave the detective a wink. "This is a great little town, Detective Kingsley. One that the Paulo Freys of this world can't destroy, no matter how hard they try. It's a lesson I learned last year."

He nodded curtly, and Odelia thought Aissa's words had touched a chord, for he gave her one of his rare smiles. "Thank you, Miss Spring."

"It's Aissa. And I hope to welcome you in our restaurant one of these nights, Detective."

"Chase, please, and I most certainly will. I can't wait to try your cuisine."

He abruptly turned and strode out, clearly wanting to avoid Odelia, but she quickly tripped after him, giving Aissa a wave. "So you managed to pin down the time of death, huh, Detective?"

But he simply kept on walking, a set look on his face.

"Did you get a cause of death, too? Detective Kingsley?"

He sped up, taking long strides that forced her to break into an awkward gait. "You can't keep ignoring me! As a reporter I have rights, you know!"

He abruptly stopped and she almost bumped into him.

"I acknowledge the fact that you have rights, Miss Poole,"

he ground out slowly, "but I, for one, don't feel obliged to honor those rights. I'm sure that whatever you need to know you can find out from your uncle, but trust me when I tell you that I intend to conduct this investigation by the book, and that doesn't include catering to the wishes of nosy reporters such as yourself."

"Well, then that's your loss, Detective!" she found herself saying, his words having pushed one button too many. "I'll have you know that I could have been a real boon to your investigation. I know this town, and everyone in it! I know this place inside out, while you're the new guy, who doesn't know a single person around here." She now found she was tapping his chest with her finger, and marveled how hard it was. The guy was built like Iron Man!

"You may know everyone in town, Miss Poole," he growled, "but I represent the law, and I intend to honor my obligation to uphold it, and not allow this investigation to turn into a town hall meeting. Good day to you." And with these words, he left her fuming on the sidewalk.

The gall of the man! Max was right. Kingsley was the spitting image of his cat: overbearing, obnoxious, and despotic. Who did he think he was, barging into town and deciding she had no business investigating a murder? She'd show him. She'd solve this murder long before he'd ferreted out his first clue. She'd show him he wasn't the hotshot detective he thought he was.

Still fuming, she resolutely set foot for the police station. Good thing her uncle wasn't as unwilling to share information as Kingsley was. She'd find out what the medical examiner had unearthed, and she'd take it from there.

CHAPTER 10

*D*ooley and I were on our way to the newspaper to tell Odelia the latest on Chase Kingsley, when I saw a familiar figure strutting along Main Street. Scratch that. When I saw *two* familiar figures strutting along Main Street as if they owned not only the street but the whole town. They were none other than Brutus and… Harriet!

"Look!" I hissed, my tail quivering in horror. "Look who's there!"

Dooley glanced over, and did a double take that practically landed him from the sidewalk into the gutter. "Oh, no! You were right, Max! Harriet is falling for that bully! No wonder she was defending him! She likes him!"

"What's not to like?" I asked bitterly. "He's an alpha male. And we all know that girls love an alpha male."

"What's an alpha male, Max?" asked Dooley.

"He's the dominant male, Dooley. The top dog."

"But Brutus is a cat, Max. How can also he be a dog?"

"It's just an expression, Dooley. It means Brutus is the one all the girls like. And obviously Harriet is one of them."

Brutus must have said something funny, for Harriet giggled loudly, and gave Brutus a gentle nudge with her shoulder. It worked on Dooley like a red flag on a bull.

"How dare he?!" he cried now. "How dare he barge in here and steal our queens! I'll teach that alpha tom!"

And before I could stop him, Dooley was stalking in the direction of the two love birds—or rather love cats.

Dutifully, I followed in his pawsteps. I couldn't very well let him handle Brutus all by himself. As his friend and house-mate I needed to have his back, like I was sure he'd have my back if something ever happened to me. It's not a strict rule with us cats, mind you. Usually we only have our own backs, and don't care too much about the rest. I mean, we're not dumb herd animals like dogs. We are solitary hunters, and used to taking care of number one. But Dooley was my buddy, and I needed to protect him from this brute.

"Dooley! Wait!" I yelled therefore, and shot across the street after him, after looking left and right. I may be a good Samaritan, but I'm not suicidal.

When I arrived on the other side of the road, Dooley was already engaging Brutus in conversation, while Harriet seemed taken aback by this sudden vehemence from our usually so placid friend.

"How dare you?!" Dooley was yelling at Brutus, even going so far as to tap him smartly on the chest. "How dare you breeze into town and take... our stuff," he lamely added with a quick glance at Harriet. "You can't do that!"

But Brutus wasn't the least bit disconcerted by this sudden sign of a local uprising. Chris Hemsworth, had he been present at the scene, hammer in hand, would have taken charge, and destroyed this interloper once and for all. But Dooley was no Thor, and Brutus had no trouble putting him in his place. "Look, little fella," he said, disdainfully swatting away Dooley's paw. "Things are going to be different around here from now on, so you better get used to it."

"Oh, is that a fact?" Dooley cried bravely.

"My human is in charge now, with your human playing second fiddle. Chase Kingsley is running this town now, and so am I, and if you want to survive under my regime, you better do as I say or else." He then turned to Harriet and added, "Come on, toots. Don't listen to this riffraff."

"Who are you calling riffraff?" I said, stepping to the fore. "Tell this cat where he can put his regime, Harriet."

"Yeah, tell him, Harriet," Dooley said. "Tell him we're your best friends and we're in charge of this place, not him."

Brutus turned to Harriet. "Remember what I promised you, sweetie pie. Fresh raw meat. An all-you-can-eat buffet of fresh raw meat. Just think what it'll do to your nice white coat. It'll be even prettier and shinier than it is now already."

Harriet's eyes glittered at the prospect of fresh raw meat, and not the kibble Marge always gave her, and she tilted her chin. "Sorry, you guys. But it looks like things are changing in this town, and either you adapt... or you perish." She shrugged. "It's a law of nature, or didn't you know?"

"But Harriet!" said Dooley, looking thoroughly confused and disappointed by this behavior from one he'd always admired from afar. Well, not afar, perhaps, as he'd been living with Harriet all his life, but you catch my drift. "You can't go with this cat. He—he—he's a... Damien!"

Brutus narrowed his eyes. "What did you call me?"

Dooley winced. "Um, Damien?"

"It's just a dumb movie," Harriet explained. "Let's go."

Brutus stared at Dooley for a few seconds more, with Dooley appearing to shrink inside his fur. Finally, content he'd once again destroyed the competition with the mere power of his presence, Brutus gave us both a grin, clicked his tongue, cocked a nail at us and strutted off with Harriet.

"It's not fair, Max," said Dooley plaintively. "He can't do this."

"Well, he just did," I said as I glared after the couple.

"But he can't just take Harriet! What's Marge gonna say?"

"Marge is going to discover a cuckoo has taken over the nest. I have a strong suspicion Brutus is extending his dominion to both our backyards."

Dooley looked up in abject alarm. "He's moving in?"

"Not moving in, exactly, as he won't want to exchange his all-you-can-eat meat buffets for Marge's kibble, but we'll be seeing a lot more of him from now on." I sighed despondently. "Face it, Dooley. Our band of three has just turned into a foursome. And judging from this preview, we won't be the top cats. More like the bottom ones."

"But I don't want to be the bottom one!"

"You're going to be, if Brutus has his way."

Dooley stared after Brutus and Harriet as they strutted their stuff, giggling and prancing like a couple of love cats.

"I like Harriet," said Dooley sadly. "I like her a lot. And I always thought that over time she'd come to like me, too."

But since there didn't seem to be much we could do about this situation, we decided to leave things be for now, and pay a visit to Odelia instead. It's a good thing that Dan always likes to leave the door to the *Gazette* offices open, so we waltzed in and went straight for Odelia's own office, where we found her checking something on her computer.

"Odelia, have we got news for you!" I announced.

"Oh, hey, Max. Dooley. I don't have a lot of time right now, you guys. I'm on my way to see Uncle Alec for an update on the murder case."

"We'll keep it brief," I promised her, and proceeded to give her a quick summary of the conversation we'd overheard between Chase and Tex. To say that she was surprised was an understatement. Apparently this was all news to her, which was gratifying. We might not be able to prevent Brutus from moving in on our territory, but at least we could still prove useful to our human's investigation.

CHAPTER 11

"*P*oole," Odelia said. "The name is Poole. Odelia Poole."

She stared annoyedly at the Mayor's secretary. The woman was new, and apparently didn't know who she was. Odelia was anxious to have a word with the Mayor's wife, who she knew had an office right next to her husband, from where she coordinated Hampton Cove's beautification committee. She needed her to confirm Aissa's story so she could take her off her suspect list.

Upon leaving the newspaper, she'd popped into the police station to have a word with Uncle Alec, but unfortunately he proved unavailable. According to Dolores he'd been summoned to the Mayor's office to give an update on the Paulo Frey case, a case destined to shake this small town to its foundations. Not only were murders pretty rare around here, but a celebrity writer being murdered was unheard of. If one celebrity got killed, it was bound to make other celebrities nervous, and soon they would start avoiding this town en masse, which was definitely bad for business.

"I'm sorry, Miss Poole," the secretary said, "but the Mayor is busy right now, and so is his wife."

She nodded, wondering whether the Mayor's wife was busy with Detective Kingsley. If he followed the same routine she did, he probably was in there questioning her right now. If only she could skip one step and go straight to the next suspect, she could get ahead of him, and solve this murder before he did. Wouldn't it be fun if he read in his morning paper who Paulo Frey's murderer was? That would make him feel pretty silly, wouldn't it?

So she decided not to wait for the Mayor's wife, and to simply assume Aissa hadn't lied about her alibi. She checked her notes, and saw that the next person to talk to was Gabby Cleret, the well-known actress.

She'd left her pickup parked in front of her dad's office, and now quickly returned there to fetch it. And as she did, she saw that her dad had stepped out of his office and was on his way back from the hardware store next door, carrying what looked like a big roll of screen.

"Hey, honey," he said when he saw her. "We keep running into each other today, don't we?"

"It's a small town, Dad," she said, then gestured at the roll of screen. "What are you up to?"

"Oh, I promised your mother I'd fix that screen door. It's been broken ever since your cat destroyed it last summer."

"My cat? Wasn't it your cat who jumped on the screen and ripped it to shreds?"

He grinned. "I think they all played an equal part in its destruction. Oh, before I forget," he said as she made to go to her pickup. "There's something I need you to do for me."

"What's that?"

"I don't know if you met him, but your uncle Alec hired a very nice new detective. His name is Chase Kingsley and he arrived in town just a couple of days ago. He's the one joining us for dinner tonight."

Her lips tightened and she crossed her arms as she leaned back against her car. "We've met."

He flashed her a grin. "Oh, that's right. Chase told me you did."

"Did he now?"

"Uh-huh. He was in here just now for a, um, consultation. The thing is, Chase used to work as a cop in New York, and got in trouble over some business out there. It's no great secret, as it was all over the New York papers a couple of months ago. He was dishonorably discharged from the NYPD," he said, also leaning against the car.

"Yes, I know," she said tersely. She could hardly tell her dad that she also knew all about the conversation he'd had with the detective in his office. It had certainly made her think. If it was true he'd been framed, it changed everything. But she hadn't made up her mind he'd been telling the truth.

A few passersby nodded friendly greetings at father and daughter Poole, and Tex greeted them back jovially. She knew exactly what her dad was going to ask her to do, and she'd been dreading the moment ever since Max and Dooley had told her about it.

"Look, I'd like to correct the impression that Chase is some kind of bad apple," said Tex. "I can't go into too much detail without divulging certain confidential information that's strictly between my patient and myself, but..."

"Just spit it out, Dad. What is it you want to tell me?"

"Chase was wronged, honey. That story about him assaulting a suspect's wife? All poppycock. So I told him I'd talk to you, Hampton Cove's premier reporter, and convince you to help spread the word that Chase Kingsley is a fine, upstanding citizen, a great cop, a credit to our community and that we're lucky to have him. And most importantly that this whole nonsense about his dismissal is simply one big misunderstanding."

"I don't know, Dad," she said, shaking her head. "Are you saying he didn't assault that woman?"

"That's exactly what I'm saying. And what Chase is saying."

"And you believe him?"

"I most certainly do."

She shook her head again. Dad was always a sucker for a sob story. Whereas she was a hard-nosed reporter, he believed anything. As she saw it, it was Chase's word against the woman he'd allegedly molested, so who was she to believe? Some far-fetched story about him catching the commissioner and Mayor Putin's wife in the act? Or the official story as it had appeared in an NYPD statement and been reported in the news? Tough choice. But judging from what she'd seen of Chase Kingsley so far, she was inclined to go with the molestation story. The guy was simply bad news.

"So what I want you to do is to write a nice little piece, extolling Chase's virtues, so to speak, and spread the rumor that his dismissal was a big mistake."

"But why would the NYPD fire a cop for no reason?"

"I, um…" Her dad quickly glanced around, then said in hushed tones, "Let's just say he saw certain things he wasn't supposed to see."

"What things?" she insisted. She wanted this on the record, so she could use it in a story if she had to.

He stared at her for a moment. "I keep forgetting what a tough reporter you are, honey. Is this the way you conduct all your interviews?"

"Of course. I'm a professional, Dad."

"Right. Um…" He scratched his scalp, clearly torn.

"I'll tell you what I heard," she said, feeling sorry for him.

"I heard Chase caught the commissioner and the Mayor's wife in the commissioner's office. Together. In a state of undress. So to make sure nobody would believe him if he talked, they bribed this suspect's wife to fabricate a story about him that got him fired. Am I close?"

He stared at her. "My God, you are good! Who told you?"

She shrugged. "I have my sources. The big question is: do you believe him?"

"Of course I do."

"What if he's lying? What if the story of him assaulting that woman is true? And this whole story about the Mayor's wife is just something he made up to protect his reputation and make sure he can work as a cop again?"

Tex shook his white-haired head. "People don't fool me that easily, honey. I've been a doctor for a long time now. Trust me, I know if they're lying or not. It's called intuition, and after so many years I've got it in spades." He stared at her. "You seem adamant to believe the worst about Chase, though. How come?"

"We met this morning in Uncle Alec's office and he took an instant dislike to me and I to him."

He waved a hand. "Oh, you got off on the wrong foot, that's all. Once you get to know him, you'll see that he's a great guy. And I'm sure a very talented police officer."

"I just wish he would let me in on the murder investigation."

"What murder investigation would this be?"

"Haven't you heard? Paulo Frey was murdered. They found his body yesterday out at the Writer's Lodge."

"The writer that disappeared last year?"

She nodded. "Dan asked me to write the story."

A smile spread across his features. "I see. And Chase doesn't want you interfering with the investigation."

"Nope. He feels reporters have no place in a murder investigation."

"Well, I can certainly understand his aversion to reporters," said Tex.

"You mean because of the hatchet piece that appeared in the *New York Post*?"

Her father nodded sagely, and gave her a grim smile. "He probably feels that that article sealed the deal on his career. Made him persona non grata."

Her dad had a point. Chase would have an ax to grind with reporters. Unless the assault charges were true. In that case he simply didn't want reporters snooping around and discovering other dark secrets from his past.

"I don't know, Dad," she said, shaking her head.

"You won't spread the story that Chase was framed?"

"I don't see how I can. Not unless I know for sure."

He sighed. "Fair enough. Always check your sources, huh?"

"Exactly. Imagine I spread the story that Chase is innocent, and it turns out that he's been playing us for a fool. That would ruin *my* reputation."

"Like I said, honey," said her father, straightening. He fixed her with a kindly look. "After all these years, nobody takes me for a fool. Trust me. But if you feel you can't do this in good conscience, then simply don't."

"You know what? I'll do a little digging. See if I can't find someone to corroborate Chase's story. If the commissioner and the Mayor's wife are having an affair, I'm sure Chase isn't the only one who knows about it."

He gave her a warm smile. "You do that, and I trust that you will uncover the truth, like you always do. In the meantime… I hope this business between you and Chase won't cause any awkwardness over dinner tonight?"

"I'll behave," she promised him. "Though I can't vouch for Detective Kingsley, Dad. The guy seems to hate me."

"He doesn't hate you, honey," her father assured her. "He's simply bitter and lashing out, that's all. Once you break bread together all will be fine."

Somehow Odelia doubted that.

CHAPTER 12

$\mathcal{O}$delia's next stop was the expansive villa of famous movie star Gabby Cleret. And as she drove there in her old Ford pickup, the one she'd bought with her first salary, she couldn't help musing on her recent talk with her dad. If it was really true that Detective Kingsley had been wrongfully accused of a crime, it wasn't enough to spread the rumor around town. He needed to be officially exonerated. Get a chance to get his old job back and get an apology from the commissioner. If—and it was a big if, she had to admit— he was right, and she found proof of this so-called affair, she wasn't going to limit herself to simply spreading a few rumors. She was going to expose the commissioner.

The longer she thought about it, the more she became convinced that perhaps there was truth to the story. She had the highest respect for both her dad and Uncle Alec, and knew both of them to be excellent judges of character. If they trusted Kingsley, maybe he was telling the truth after all. Which meant he'd been the victim of a terrible crime, and justice had to be done. She'd always abhorred injustice, and now started to see her story taking a completely different direction. Instead of exposing the detective, perhaps she needed to expose the ones who'd got him kicked off the force?

She arrived at the oceanfront property of Gabby Cleret, just outside Hampton Cove, located on one of those pieces of prime real estate that had long ago been snapped up by the more wealthy residents of the Hamptons.

Like Detective Kingsley, Gabby had moved to Hampton Cove in a bid to escape the fallout of a scandal that had cost her her career. The details were a little fuzzy, but she seemed to remember she'd starred in a remake of *Raiders of the Lost Ark*, only with a female lead this time to take over Harrison Ford's iconic role. It hadn't gone down well with fanboys the world over, who'd viciously attacked both her and the picture, and had managed to destroy them both.

Apparently so-called fans hadn't taken too kindly to their favorite movie being recast with a woman this time, and a plus-sized woman at that, and had been quite vocal about it, bombarding the movie and its star with all manner of vile abuse, with Gabby bearing the brunt of the attack. The actress had taken it badly, especially after the movie had tanked spectacularly, and had lost the studio hundreds of millions, causing her career to stall. She hadn't made another movie since, hiding from the storm out here in the Hamptons, and licking her wounds.

Odelia had met Gabby once, and had even interviewed her for the *Hampton Cove Gazette*. They'd gotten along great, and Odelia hoped she'd remember her and would be willing to talk about the Paulo Frey business.

Ten minutes after she'd rung the bell, she was sipping from a cup of tea out on the deck, while Gabby sniffed from a bouquet of roses a fan and admirer had apparently left on the porch. They were looking out across the pool area, which was now covered with a tarp, and the ocean beyond.

"Nice place you got here, Gabby," she said appreciatively.

"Yeah, it's my own little piece of paradise," Gabby confirmed with a tired smile. She looked a little under the weather, Odelia thought, and more subdued than the boisterous woman she remembered, both from the movie and her personal experience when they'd spent a fun afternoon together.

Gabby Cleret was an attractive woman in her mid-thirties, with an expressive face and long black hair that she'd pulled up high into a bun. A long, loose-fitting robe hid her cuddly figure. She wasn't one of those skinny stars, and had never made excuses for her more womanly curves. It was one more reason the fanboys had singled her out for abuse, as apparently a woman wasn't allowed to have curves and had to look like a stick figure.

"I actually came here to ask you about Paulo Frey," Odelia finally said.

She saw how Gabby visibly stiffened. "What about him?" she asked, her smile quickly evaporating.

"I don't know if anyone told you this, but his body was found yesterday, buried out at the Writer's Lodge. He was murdered."

Gabby's eyebrows shot up. "Murdered? Are you sure?"

"Looks like it. I'm doing a piece for the *Gazette*, and I was talking to Aissa Spring just now, who told me you had some kind of run-in with the guy?"

Gabby nodded, gazing out across the ocean for a moment, then fixing her dark eyes back on Odelia. "He was a mean man, Odelia. A real mean man."

"I gathered that from Aissa's story."

"He tried to destroy her restaurant, just because Marissa has curves. He tried to destroy me for the same reason, and also because I was a woman playing a man's part. He said I was simply too ugly to be in the movies, spoiling things for movie buffs like him. He said that in Hollywood's glory days a woman like me would never have been allowed to star in a movie."

"Too ugly? He said that?"

"He called me dogface. And he didn't just say it, he wrote it, in a bombardment of tweets aimed at me, enthusiastically retweeted by his posse of followers. It turned into this toxic thing," she said, shaking her head, "and caused the story to move away from the movie to my personal appearance." She sniffed one of the roses again, and seemed to take comfort in the sweet fragrance.

"That must have been horrible," Odelia said commiserat- ingly. The more she heard about Paulo Frey, the more it appeared the man was some kind of monster.

"His followers didn't just attack me, they attacked the movie, too. They launched so many one-star reviews on the movie's IMDb page that it had an actual effect on attendance figures, greatly exacerbated by their boycott."

"But why? Why go to all that trouble just for a stupid movie?" asked Odelia. "I mean, no offense. I saw the movie and I loved it, especially your performance. I think you did a great job and you were perfect for the part."

"Thanks," said Gabby with a smile. "I didn't get it either. Not then, not now. All I can think is that Paulo Frey hated women of size. He thought the studio should never have replaced Harrison Ford with me and seemed to consider it a personal insult and so did a lot of his followers. Basically he decided to cancel me."

"He did a pretty good job by the looks of it."

"He did. Not only did he singlehandedly manage to destroy the movie, losing the studio hundreds of millions, and sink a potential franchise, he also destroyed my career. There were supposed to be two more films, but those will never be made, and I haven't received a decent script since."

She produced a mirthless laugh. "He got exactly what he wanted: he destroyed my career and my life."

"But you can't let one guy do that to you, Gabby," Odelia said. "You're a talented, beautiful woman. You can't let this horrible thing define your life. I'm sure if you go back out there you'll see there are plenty of people who adore you and your work. You have brought so much joy to the world."

"That's very nice of you to say, Odelia," said Gabby gratefully, "but I don't know if you're right. It wasn't much fun going through such an experience and frankly I'm afraid that it will happen again and destroy me."

"Well," she said, "the ringleader is gone, so there's that. He can't hurt you anymore." Which reminded her. "Um, I have to ask you this, Gabby, but do you have any idea where you were on the night of September sixteen last year?"

Gabby laughed. "You're asking me for my alibi? Why? Do you think I killed Frey? I didn't even know he was in town. If I had, I'd never have bought a house here."

"He stayed at the Writer's Lodge every year, to write his books."

"Good thing we never bumped into each other. I might have killed him."

She eyed the other woman uncertainly. "But you didn't, right?"

"Of course not! Do I look like a murderer? The only thing I've killed is a production company, and even that wasn't my fault but Paulo Frey's."

"The company went belly up?" She made a quick note of that.

"Yes, it did. Look, I'm not going to lie to you and tell you I'm not happy that the man is dead, but I can promise you I wasn't the one who did it. Now where's my phone?" She searched around until she'd located her smartphone and snatched it from the side table that held, amongst other things, a voluminous tome that appeared to be *Lord of the Rings*. Odelia saw that the screensaver on her phone was the movie poster for the Indiana Jones movie. The actress slipped a pair of half-moon glasses onto her nose and checked the phone, her long-nailed fingers clicking on the glass. She called up the calendar app and squinted at the screen. "I was in LA that weekend," she finally said. "Ironically enough to be told the news that the sequel to *Raiders of the Lost Ark* had been canceled after the first picture sank like a stone at the box office. So there," she said, placing down the phone. "I didn't kill Frey but I heartily commend whoever did. They rid the world of a great evil."

"Thanks, Gabby," she said, getting up. "And think about what I said." She placed her hand on her heart. "Your fans miss you. I miss you. Your place is out there, amongst your true fans, of which you have many, I promise you."

Gabby gave her a grateful smile and they shared a quick hug. "Thanks, honey," she said. "Maybe now that Frey is dead, I can show my face again. And maybe even make movies again."

They both laughed as Gabby escorted her through the house and into a marble atrium. She opened the front door and was surprised to find a tall man standing before her, his finger poised over the bell button.

"Detective Kingsley," she said sweetly. "I was just leaving." She gestured to Gabby. "She's all yours, but I can tell you already that she didn't do it, and that her alibi is rock solid." And with these words, she slipped past the cop, who looked absolutely dumbfounded, and gave Gabby a pinky wave before sashaying down the front steps and making her way to her truck, parked in the circular driveway. In the battle between the *Hampton Cove Gazette* and the Hampton Cove PD, it was obvious she was way ahead.

CHAPTER 13

"*Y*ou know, one good thing about Harriet getting involved with Brutus is that he'll be so busy showing off to her he won't bother us," I told Dooley as we sat on the little patio behind the *Gazette*, grooming and basking in the sun.

Dooley and I might not be the most handsome cats around, but that didn't mean we didn't take our grooming seriously. Every cat worth his or her salt likes to preen, and we were no exceptions.

We weren't alone, as the *Gazette's* owner, Dan Goory, was rocking in his rocking chair, going over the proofs of one of his articles. The old man liked to sit here and take a load off his feet, and occasionally smoke a cigar. We always made sure we sat upwind from him, as we weren't too keen on the smell. Sometimes Dan and Odelia would sit there together and discuss the next day's edition of the *Gazette*. It was better than being cooped up inside.

"I don't know," said Dooley between two licks. "I'm sure he'll manage to fit bullying us into his busy schedule, Max."

"I don't think so. In fact I'm pretty sure that as long as

those two are an item, he'll leave us in peace," I said, trying to lift my friend's mood. He'd been feeling downcast after making the discovery that the cat he'd been sweet on for so many years had fallen for the new cat on the block.

"I hope you're right," said Dooley, giving his tail a tentative lick and then, deciding it was clean enough, leaving it for another time. "Let's hope that as long as Brutus is stepping out with Harriet we're safe from his bullying ways."

"Which means we can do whatever we want. Go wherever we like and generally be masters of our own fate again without that brute interfering."

"So what do you want to do?"

I thought for a moment. What did I want to do? I wanted to solve this murder, that's what I wanted to do. And make sure Odelia got the scoop. I liked this small town, and I didn't like it when people started murdering each other. It wasn't nice. And since violence tends to lead to more violence, someone had to put a stop to it before things got out of hand. At least that's how I saw it.

"We could hang out at the barbershop," Dooley suggested.

It was one of our favorite haunts. You'd be surprised what kind of secrets people tell their barber. Almost as many as they divulge to their doctor.

"Why don't we head out to the lodge and see if we can't pick up the scent of the killer?" I suggested instead. The barbershop could wait. We were born hunters, after all, and perhaps we could pick up the scent of the murderer.

Dooley brightened, and I saw that this would be good for him. It would keep his mind off Brutus and Harriet strutting their stuff along Main Street. "That's a great idea, Max," he said enthusiastically. "Maybe we can sniff out the killer and then all Odelia has to do is make them confess."

"Let's do this," I said, and we bumped fists.

It's called teamwork, people, and it's not just humans that

do it. Dooley and I have been living together for so many years we make a pretty great team. What's more, we've grown attached to our humans, and like to help them out. When it suits us, of course. We're not dogs, after all!

So we left Dan on the back porch marking up his articles with a deep frown on his face, and trotted off, setting paw for the Writer's Lodge. One disadvantage of being a cat is that we don't get to drive a car. Or a bike. Which means we have to go everywhere on paw. But like I said, we're natural born hunters, and what are a couple of miles for your friendly neighborhood predator? Chicken feed. Still, after we'd been on the move for a while, I was starting to wonder if this was such a good idea after all.

"Are we there yet?" asked Dooley, panting slightly.

"No idea, buddy, but I hope so. My paws are killing me."

"And mine. What's more, I'm getting tired, Max."

"I'm sure it won't be much longer now."

We walked on in silence for a couple of minutes. We'd left the heart of town behind, and were now traipsing through the woods. This piece of the trail was all uphill, and I wondered who would voluntarily go and live in the middle of nowhere just so they could write a book? Nuts.

"You know? When this is all over and we've caught the killer, maybe we'll get a nice treat," said Dooley. "Like that raw meat Brutus gets from Chase?"

"I doubt it," I said. "All we ever get are leftovers, and they're cooked."

"Maybe when Brutus comes to live with us he'll share his meals?"

"Dream on, buddy. Brutus doesn't strike me as the sharing type."

"You're probably right. And if he shares, it'll be with Harriet, not us."

We scaled a small hill, and passed beneath some brambles,

to come out on the other side looking like pincushions. We shed the prickles and trudged on.

"What does Brutus have that we don't?" Dooley asked suddenly.

I sighed. "Is this about Harriet again?"

"It's about Brutus being treated like royalty."

"Well, Brutus is a pedigree cat, Dooley. They are like royalty. While we're just your average alley cats that got picked out of the litter by an indiscriminate hand. I'm sure that when Chase got Brutus, he paid good money for that cat, while we're lucky we didn't end up at the pound."

"So he's a prize-winning cat and we're just a bunch of ugly mongrels?" Dooley said bitterly. Maybe this hike wasn't such a good idea, after all. Instead of taking his mind off Brutus and Harriet, it seemed to have the opposite effect.

"Pretty much," I agreed. "Though I wouldn't call you a mongrel, Dooley. Or ugly."

"But it's true, isn't it? Brutus has probably won a ton of cat shows."

I shuddered at the thought of having to compete in a cat show. "It's only natural that after paying top dollar for Brutus, Chase would want to show him off," I speculated. "Which is probably why he feeds him a diet of raw meat."

"Hey, maybe we should enter a cat show," said Dooley. "Show Odelia that we're special, too. Maybe then she'll start feeding us raw meat."

"I doubt whether we'd stand a chance," I said, shaking my head at so much naiveté. As if we could ever compete with the likes of Brutus.

"Why not?" he asked. "It worked for Babe, didn't it?"

I frowned. "Babe? Who's Babe?"

"Don't you remember that movie we saw the other night? About a piglet that grows up on a farm, and the farmer trains him to be a sheepdog? And since he was so nice and polite all the sheep loved him and did exactly what he told them to do at the animal show? He didn't even have to bark at them or bite them or any of that stuff. So if Babe can do it, so can we."

"Do what, exactly? Become sheepdogs?"

"Not sheepdogs, Max," he said with a laugh. "Perform at a cat show!"

Become a cat model? Never! "I really don't think so, Dooley."

"But we're special, Max, just like Babe. I just know we are."

"Look, that was a Hollywood movie. In Hollywood movies animals are always special. Penguins have happy feet and pigs can corral sheep and cats eat lasagna and sound like Bill Murray. In real life? Not so much."

"But we can talk. We can talk to Odelia. And to Marge. And Gran." He gave me a grin. "I'm sure that Brutus can't talk to Chase."

Well, that was true enough. Brutus might get prime chops, but I doubted whether he could chat with his human. Dooley and I might not be pedigree cats, or have the appeal of a sheepherding pig or dancing penguins, but we could help Odelia solve this murder, and that definitely made us special.

We'd arrived at the Writer's Lodge, and saw that the place was completely cordoned off with crime scene tape, the yellow kind.

"Come on," I said as I followed the scent of human excrement. "Over there."

We hurried to the place where the crime had been committed and stopped at the demolished structure that had formerly been the outhouse. The entire thing had been taken apart, the boards piled up high next to a sizable hole dug into the earth. A small crane stood parked next to it, which had probably been used to get the body of the murdered writer out of the hole. When we took a tentative peek into the abyss, I saw it was pretty deep. And smelled terrible.

"Yuck," I said. "This stench is hard to bear."

Unlike humans, cats can't pinch their noses, which are a lot more sensitive to begin with, so the foul stench emanating from the former latrine was an assault on my senses that was worse than I'd imagined. Generations of writers had used that pit, and so had generations of Hampton Covians, as the Writer's Lodge outhouse was as popular with the locals as it was with writers. When nature suddenly called, hikers had the choice between relieving themselves in the bushes or the outhouse. But why wipe your tush with a piece of bark or a clump of grass when you could use Hetta Fried's velvet comfort triple-layered toilet paper instead? After all, what's good enough for bestselling writers is good enough for the local yokels.

Luckily for the lodge's paying guests, they got preferential treatment. So when a desperate hiker came running, and found the outhouse occupied by a writer, they simply had to hold and wait until the scribbler had done their business before adding their own contribution.

"So this is where they found the guy, huh?" asked Dooley, his face twisted in a grimace as he tried to endure the horrible stench.

"Yeah. Looks like," I croaked.

The pit had been completely emptied out, and I couldn't even see the bottom, nor did I feel inclined to jump in and investigate.

"Do you smell the killer?" asked Dooley, gagging a little.

"I definitely smell something, but it's not the killer," I wheezed, and quickly removed myself from the scene.

And that's when I bumped into another cat who was lurking around. I recognized her as one of the wild felines that like to roam these woods, and live as nature has intended it: free and untethered, roaming the earth alone.

"Hey, Clarice," I said by way of greeting. "So what are you doing here?"

Clarice, who is skinny, with gray hair matted and twisted in knots, had a wild look in her eyes. She is feral, and we usually try to avoid her. But this was not a regular social call. We needed answers and we needed them fast and maybe Clarice had seen something out there.

"Do you have any idea who killed this writer person?" asked Dooley, who'd joined me. The stench had become too much for him as well. At least where we lived, humans used a flush toilet, and the smell never gets as bad as out there, where they still adhere to a more primitive waste disposal method.

"I saw nothing," said Clarice now in a vicious snarl.

"You mean you weren't around when the murder happened?" I asked.

She shook her head. "I saw nothing."

"Maybe you saw this Paulo Frey character when he was still alive. He was a regular at the Writer's Lodge, right?" I asked, probing a little further.

She stared at me, looking more feral than ever. It gave me the creeps. The longer Clarice lived out there, the weirder she seemed to get.

"I saw nothing," she repeated a third time, sticking to her story no matter what. And then, before we could continue our line of questioning, she simply darted away, and shot off into the woods, as if fired from a gun, afraid we might push her to reach deep and way beyond her limited vocabulary.

"That was a little weird," said Dooley.

"Yeah, not very helpful," I admitted.

We both stuck our noses in the air, to see if we couldn't pick up any scent, and discovered we could pick up plenty of them. Too many, in fact, as it appeared half of Hampton Cove had been out there, which didn't surprise me. Everyone wanted to take a peek at that crime scene, and find out for themselves what was going on.

"I think this was a waste of time," Dooley finally said.

Just then, I pricked up my ears, for I'd heard the engine of a car whine in the distance, working hard to haul a car up these hills and join us. "Did you hear that?" I asked.

"Someone's coming," Dooley said. Then his eyes widened. "Oh! Do you think it's the killer? They always say killers return to the scene of the crime!"

"The crime's been committed over a year ago, Dooley. Why would the killer wait until now to show up?"

"Because it's taken until now for the body to be discovered!"

I had to concede he had a point, and we waited with bated breath for the killer to show his or her face. But the car that finally made it up the steep incline was a very familiar one, and we both shared a happy grin.

"Great," said Dooley. "We can hitch a ride back with Odelia."

For it was indeed our human's very own old Ford pickup that now crested the final stretch of road before the lodge, and hove into view.

Odelia stepped from the truck's cabin and tentatively looked around. When she saw us sauntering from the shrubbery, she smiled. "Hey, you guys. What are you doing all the way out here?"

"We just thought we'd take a closer look at the crime scene," I said as I curled myself around her leg and butted my head against her calf.

"We thought we'd sniff out the killer," Dooley added.

"And? Any luck?" she asked as she crouched down and

scratched our necks. We both purred with contentment, our tails gently quivering.

"Lots of scents," I said. "But hard to determine which one's the killer's."

"I don't think you'll be able to isolate the killer's scent," she said. "The crime was committed a long time ago. Lots of people have been here since."

"So what are you doing out here?" I asked.

Odelia tapped her smartphone smartly. "Taking a couple of pictures for my article." She walked over to what was left of the outhouse and started snapping pictures, making sure she got it from all the different angles.

"Are you any closer to solving the murder?" asked Dooley.

"Nope," she said, walking back to us. "I talked to two women who had a run-in with Paulo Frey, and they both told me what a dreadful man he was. Really spiteful and mean. It seems he hated persons of size, and especially plus-sized women, and liked to harass them and try to destroy them."

"Sounds like a nice guy," I said as I watched Odelia approach the lodge to take a couple of snaps there. It was a fairly small structure, completely constructed from dark oak, with a nice verandah, where Hetta had installed the Jacuzzi. Writers enjoyed soaking in the hot tub while experiencing the great outdoors and gazing up at the stars twinkling above. If it didn't inspire them to write the great American novel, at least they got to enjoy a good soak in the hot tub.

"So no leads?" asked Dooley.

"Well, the two women I talked to both had alibis, so that was a dead end, but it made me think…"

"Yes?" I asked encouragingly.

She paused, a frown appearing on her smooth brow. "If Frey was the kind of man they said he was, and I don't doubt they were telling me the truth, he must have made other enemies. And maybe one of them finally decided enough was enough and put a stop to the harassment. Permanently."

She walked around to the other side of the lodge, snapping more pictures. And that's when I heard another car pulling up.

"Uh-oh," I said, alarmed. "Looks like we've got company."

"The killer!" cried Dooley.

I checked the car that now appeared over the rim. "Close, but no cigar."

CHAPTER 14

$\mathcal{O}$delia was wondering how to get inside the lodge. She wanted to take a few snaps of the place where Frey had spent his final hours, to add color to the story and set the scene. She should have asked Hetta for the key before driving out there, but it had been one of those spur-of-the-moment kind of things. When she couldn't reach her uncle, she'd figured she might as well drive up and soak up the atmosphere. Get a feel for the place. She rattled the doorknob in frustration. Nope. That one was locked. Then she noticed that a window on the second floor was open, probably to air out the place.

Tucking away her smartphone, she quickly climbed one of the trellises that reached from the ground floor all the way up to the roof, and hopped onto the black slate roof, from where she started making her way to the window. Her tongue sticking out, she was just wondering what she'd say if anyone caught her breaking and entering, when a familiar voice sounded behind her.

"What do you think you're doing up there, Miss Poole?"

She looked down, and saw she'd been joined by none

other than Detective Kingsley. He was staring up at her, his expression implacable.

"What are *you* doing here?" she shot back. "And how is it that wherever I go, I bump into you? Are you following me, Detective Kingsley?"

"I asked you first," he said. "Why do you insist on sticking your nose into my investigation? Interviewing my witnesses? Disturbing my crime scene?"

"It's called journalism, Detective," she said. "It's what reporters do."

"This is a crime scene," he repeated, that same set look on his face she'd seen every time they'd met. "You can't go traipsing all over the place."

"Well, you're doing it," she challenged, "so I don't see why I can't."

"I'm in charge of this investigation," he pointed out. "So I'll ask you again: what are you doing up there, Miss Poole?"

"I, um…" She'd started making her way down from the roof. She now saw she should have worn jeans that morning, and not this silly little dress. She had the impression that Detective Kingsley could see her pink undies from where he was standing, and that was the absolute last thing she needed right now. "I just wanted to find an original angle on the place where the body was found." She gestured at the outhouse. "I figured I'd have a great shot from up here."

But as she was descending the roof, her foot slipped on a slick patch, and she suddenly was hurtling down a lot quicker than she'd anticipated. She cried out when she reached the roof's edge and scrambled for support. Her fingers caught a clump of wet leaves and she lost purchase and tumbled over the edge, on a collision course with the unyielding ground below.

Just as she braced for impact, however, she was snatched in midair by two strong arms that caught her just in time.

And she suddenly found herself in such close proximity with the hardened cop that she felt like a little bird falling from its nest and being caught by some creature of the wild.

She was at his mercy now, and could feel her heart beating wildly against her breastbone, the Detective's face so close she could see tiny flecks of green in his icy blue eyes, and the slight stubble that dusted his cheeks. His arms were strong and powerful, and for a moment she had the distinct impression there might be kissing in her immediate future.

But as quickly as he'd caught her, he released her again, by returning her to perpendicularity, setting her down so gently she surprised herself by heaving out a soft sigh. He then pointed at the green smudges on her dress.

"You'll have to get that dry-cleaned," he grumbled, giving her a hard look.

She was still panting slightly, her heart racing, and she knew it wasn't from the drop but from being in such close proximity with the Detective's hard chest. She hadn't been this close to a man for a while, her last boyfriend having fled Hampton Cove over a year ago, when he'd been caught embezzling funds from the local bank. Sam had been a teller and had both swindled the bank out of a nice sum of money and her out of her illusions.

He'd been a nice young man, and she'd even brought him home to meet her parents and grandmother for dinner. He'd been nothing like Chase Kingsley, who, she now realized, was an actual man, while Sam was a boy.

"I, um, thank you," she finally managed. His hands were still expertly removing a few leaves from her person. Her lips tightened and she stepped back. "Thank you for saving my life, Detective Kingsley."

"I don't think I saved your life, Miss Poole," he said, also straightening, "but you're welcome. And now I think it's time for you to head back into town."

Anger flared inside her. Who did he think he was ordering her around like this? Maybe it was time she put him in his place. "I'm actually doing a story on you as well, Detective. A story my readers will find fascinating."

"Is that so?" he asked, eyeing her a little wearily.

"Oh, yes. Lots of rumors have been swirling around about you, and I think it's important to separate fact from fiction. Set the record straight."

"As a matter of fact, that's exactly what I think, too," he admitted.

"So… would you like to comment on your dismissal from the NYPD?"

Instantly, his expression hardened. "You know very well that was a hatchet piece that appeared in the *New York Post*. No truth to the story whatsoever."

"All I know is that you were accused of molesting a suspect's wife, and that she filed charges against you, which caused your immediate dismissal."

His eyes suddenly blazed with fury. "That story was a fabrication and a lie," he growled. "Nothing about it was even remotely true."

"Then you won't mind setting the record straight? Give the good people of Hampton Cove your version of the facts?"

"It's not my *version* of the facts, Miss Poole. They *are* the facts."

"And what are those? And why haven't you told them to anyone before?"

At this, instead of launching into a long-winded harangue about the Mayor's wife and the commissioner, as she'd expected, he simply closed his mouth with a click, and stood there glaring at her.

"Oh, come on, Detective Kingsley," she prompted. "You can do better than that." She took a step closer. "Isn't it, in fact, true that you claim you stumbled upon a secret liaison between the commissioner and the Mayor's wife? That you were consequently the victim of a cover-up, and that these false accusations leveled against you were simply a way of discrediting you so no one would believe your crazy story about the commissioner's illicit affair?"

His face had taken on a darker tinge of scarlet. A vein was dangerously throbbing at his temple, and she took another step closer.

"Where did you hear that?" he finally demanded in a deep, low growl.

She shrugged. "I'm a professional, Detective. I have my sources."

When he grabbed her by the shoulders, she knew she'd gone too far. "Tell me who told you about this," he spat, his eyes boring into hers with an intensity that held her spellbound.

"I-I can't," she said, suddenly realizing the dangerous position she'd maneuvered herself in. Here she was, all alone in the woods, near the scene where Paulo Frey had been murdered, with a cop who stood accused of molesting a woman and had lost his job as a consequence. Why did she have to come out here alone? And why did she have to provoke this man? She'd poked the bear, and now he was awake and furious and ready to devour her!

"I want you to let me go now," she said, squirming.

"Not before you tell me who told you about the commissioner."

"I can't and I won't!"

He shook her again. "Was it your father? Did he tell you?"

"Of course not! I—everyone knows the story. It's all over town!"

He stared at her at this, aghast. "All over town?"

"Yes! It's not a secret, if that's what you think."

He was still staring at her, his face ashen now. She wriggled out of his arms, and this time he let go, looking absolutely shell-shocked.

"And let me tell you that I, for one, don't believe a word of it," she said. "That whole story about the Mayor's wife? I think you made that up. I think you're a brute and you went too far that day and you did in fact molest that poor woman."

He blinked, finally coming out of his stupor when her words hit him. Surprised, she watched as a look of torment came over his face. "We're done here, Miss Poole," he said in a voice so quiet she had to strain her ears to pick up the words. "We're done," he said, then started to walk away from her, his back straight, his shoulders stiff and his demeanor unreadable.

And as she watched him walk away, she realized what she'd done. The only two people in town he'd entrusted with his secret were her father and her uncle. In Chase's mind one of them must have betrayed his confidence. How else could she have known? And now he would probably never trust them again. She'd really done it this time. Maybe he'd even resign and leave Hampton Cove because of her. Chase Kingsley was obviously a proud man, and might simply walk away.

"Detective!" she called out, and hurried after him. "Chase! Come back!"

She caught up with him just as he reached his car, a pickup like hers, but a much shinier model. He whirled around. "What?" he asked, his jaw working.

"I, um…" She didn't know what to say for a moment. How could she explain that she got all of her information from her cat? That was simply ludicrous. But how else could she have known? In his mind her father had broken his trust, or her uncle. She needed to tell him the truth, no matter how improbable it might sound. Or… "I'll tell you where I heard the story."

"I know. All over town," he gritted out.

"No! No, I'm the only one who knows. And… and Beah."

He stared at her, his face inscrutable, and folded his massive arms across his chest, leaning against the truck. He wasn't giving her an inch. "Go on."

"I… I worked for the *New York Post* for six months, as an intern, right after I finished college. I didn't like it out there, though, and quickly decided to return to Hampton Cove, where Dan had always promised me a position on his paper. He was getting on in years, and couldn't do it all by himself anymore. The work maybe wasn't as exciting as working for one of the big papers, but it was exactly what I wanted. But while I was interning at the *Post* I became close to another intern. Beah Heaves and I became friends, and even after I returned here we kept in touch. We, um, we exchange information. When she needs help on a story about the Hamptons, or I need something on New York, we help each other out."

"So?" he grunted, his eyes remaining steadily on hers.

"Well, I called her this morning, asking about you, and she told me the story about the harassment, and…" She hesitated, licking her lips. "She also told me that a crazy rumor had done the rounds that you were set up. That the harassment charge was simply a way to make you go away."

His frown deepened. "If this reporter friend of yours knew about this, why didn't she pursue the story? Why was this never printed in her paper?"

She lifted an ineffectual hand. "Isn't it obvious? Because nobody believed the rumors. They figured you started them yourself, to get off the hook."

He shifted, giving her a slight nod. "And what do you believe?"

She cast around helplessly. To be honest, she hadn't made up her mind yet.

She didn't have to, for his jaw worked when he growled, "I see."

And then he abruptly turned and yanked open the door of his car and slid behind the wheel. When he turned back to her, his face was a mask of determination. "Just make sure that when you print your story you make sure to get a quote from the commissioner this time. Get him on record."

"Why?" she asked, surprised.

"Because he's never actually come out openly and accused me of a crime." He gave her a grim-faced look. "Just ask him the question straight to his face, and see how he responds. I'm sure a big-shot reporter like yourself will have no trouble recognizing a blatant lie when you hear it."

With these words, he started up the truck and the engine roared to life. Before she had a chance to respond, he was racing away, wheels spinning and leaving her in a cloud of dust and wondering what she'd gotten herself into this time.

For some reason, she was starting to believe that Chase Kingsley just might be telling the truth after all, which meant she'd been wrong all along.

CHAPTER 15

*D*ooley and I rode in the back in silence for a while, as Odelia seemed to ponder Chase's words. She now had two cases on her plate: a nasty murder, and the mystery of the new cop, and seemed determined to solve both. Dooley had stretched himself out on the backseat and was already snoring softly, while I was gazing at the back of Odelia's head, wondering what else we could do for her. It was obvious the recent meeting with Chase hadn't gone well, and judging from her silence it had made a great impact.

I wondered why this was. Why would this Detective Kingsley cause her so much distress? She'd gone toe to toe with people before—these things happen when you're a tough-as-nails reporter—and she'd shrugged off those incidents in a heartbeat. This time the confrontation had left an indelible impression, and I thought I knew why this was. The same reason Harriet had fallen so unexpectedly for Brutus: this new cop was an alpha male. The kind of male that made a powerful impact on the female of the species.

I'd seen it before and I recognized the signs: Odelia was

developing feelings for this detective, even though she probably didn't know it herself.

Why else would she care whether Chase Kingsley was innocent in this whole harassment business or not? If he were simply some Mr. Nobody she would have dismissed him out of hand, but now she was almost as eager to solve his mystery as she was to solve the Paulo Frey murder.

And then I got an idea. I know, it sometimes happens, even to cats. I don't know where these sudden moments of illumination come from, but I'm grateful when they come. And no, I'm not saying I'm the smartest cat around, because I'm not, but I do have my moments, if I say so myself.

"Hey," I said, deftly hopping onto the passenger seat. "I've got an idea."

"Mh?" asked Odelia without looking up. She was still deep in thought as she steered her pickup expertly down the winding road back into town.

"You want to find out if Chase is innocent, right?"

This time she did look up, and gave me a sideways glance. "Yes? So?"

"Well, if the commissioner and the Mayor's wife are having a torrid affair, it's bound to have spilled over from his office to other places as well, right?"

"Probably," she agreed.

"I mean, if the flames of passion have been fanned that high, they won't be able to confine themselves to his office."

She laughed at his. "I don't know if this is an appropriate conversation for a young cat like yourself, Max."

I puffed up my chest. "Young cat? Haven't you ever heard of cat years? I'm not a spring chicken. I'm a grown-up. I can handle this stuff."

"All right," she said with a slight smile. "So what's your big idea?"

"Well, it's not as if you can walk up to the commissioner and ask him point blank if he's having an affair with the Mayor's wife, right?"

"No, I don't think that's such a good idea," she agreed with a grimace.

"What are you guys talking about?" asked Dooley from the backseat. He'd woken up and was yawning cavernously, inspiring me to follow suit.

"Max has got an idea," said Odelia.

"Of course he has," said Dooley, joining me on the front seat. "Max is very clever. He always has lots of great ideas."

"Thanks, buddy," I said. "So like I was telling Odelia, if the commissioner and the Mayor's wife are having an affair, someone is bound to have noticed."

"Someone?" asked Odelia. "I doubt that very much, Max. I'm sure they're very careful to hide their affair."

"Did I say 'someone'? I meant 'some cat,' of course. Whatever humans do, there's usually a cat around, as there's so many of us, and humans tend not to notice we're there half the time. They don't realize we're everywhere—and we like to blab."

"Oh, do we like to blab," Dooley confirmed, stolidly licking his paws.

"We blab a lot."

"All the time."

"So there you have it!" I said triumphantly, settling back to collect my well-deserved round of applause.

But Odelia didn't seem convinced. "I don't get it. What are you saying?"

I frowned at her. Sometimes I wonder if human intelligence is as well-developed as they seem to think it is. "I'm saying that there's bound to be a cat out there who has seen something, and since all cats blab, probably the entire cat community of New York knows about this by now, and since cats also like to wander around, word has probably reached beyond the city limits and might even have traveled as far as Hampton Cove."

"So all we need to do now," added Dooley, "is to find a cat who knows a cat who's seen a cat who knows a cat—"

"Yes, yes," I said, stemming the flow of words. "What Dooley means is that we need to find a cat who knows a cat who's seen—"

"Hey! That's what I said!" exclaimed Dooley.

"No, it's not," I argued.

"It is, too!"

"Not!"

"You guys!" Odelia cried, laughing. "I get the picture. So you're telling me you're willing to look into this whole Chase Kingsley harassment case?"

"That's exactly what I'm saying," I said.

"And what I'm saying too," Dooley said.

Odelia glanced at us. "It's very sweet of you to offer, but I don't know…"

"Well, I do," I said. "Not that we need to, mind you, cause us cats have a sixth sense so we already know if Chase Kingsley is telling the truth or not."

Her eyes widened. "Oh? So *is* he telling the truth?"

I stared at her, not sure how to respond. I knew a lot depended on my answer. For one thing, if she started dating this Chase person, like humans tend to do, our lives would never be the same again. Sooner or later she'd get involved with the guy, him being an alpha male and all, and then Brutus would become part of our extended family, which would turn our lives into hell. On the other hand, if it was Chase she wanted, it was Chase she should get, for deep down I thought he probably wasn't as bad as all that. And God knows that Odelia deserved to get herself a decent guy for once, especially after that Sam creep she had dated last time. Dooley and I had warned her that he was up to something, but she hadn't listened, and not only had he turned out to be a creep, but a nasty thief, too.

"Look, I'll tell you what I think, but on one condition," I finally said.

"What's that?" she asked tensely.

"Yeah, what's that, Max?" Dooley chimed in.

"You have to do something about Brutus!"

"Max has a point," Dooley admitted. "Something needs to be done about Brutus. If he's going to live with us he needs to be told to behave."

Odelia stared at us. "Brutus living with us? What are you talking about?"

I sighed. "You know as well as we do that you like this Chase guy. And so once you guys move in together and start nesting and making babies, Brutus will become a fixture. The only way to take him down a peg is to talk to him."

"And talk tough," said Dooley. "A very tough talk."

To my surprise, Odelia burst out laughing.

"Hey, this is not a joke!" I reminded her. "Our lives are at stake here."

"Our very lives," Dooley echoed.

"You really think that Chase and I…" She shook her head, still laughing. "So you actually think that Chase and I are going to move in together?"

"Of course! Isn't it obvious? You like the guy and he likes you, so you're bound to end up together at some point in the future. I know humans, Odelia. I've studied the species extensively. I know instant attraction when I see it."

She was still shaking her head, her blond hair dangling around her shoulders. She looked lovely, I thought. Sunlight slanted in through the grimy windshield and lit up her features, and made her hair shine golden. No wonder Chase couldn't keep from bumping into her wherever she went.

"Look, Max. I don't know what you think you saw, but Chase and I are never going to become an item. He doesn't even like me. In fact he hates me. And I…" She faltered, and then said stubbornly, "Well, I don't like him a lot either."

"Yeah, yeah. Just keep telling yourself that. Anyway, here's the deal: promise to have a long talk with Brutus and I'll tell you what kind of guy Chase Kingsley really is."

"All right. If Chase and I should ever get together—and that's a very big if—I'll talk to his cat Brutus and tell him to behave from now on. How does that sound?"

"Great," I said, the prospect of Brutus being taken down a peg or two suddenly putting me in a great mood. Hey, I never said we're always the cuddly, sweet-tempered creatures you humans seem to think we are!

"Now tell me," she insisted. "Is Chase innocent of these harassment charges like he claims, or is he simply lying through his teeth?"

She gazed at me expectantly, and I gave her a reassuring grin, though I doubt whether she could spot it. "He's innocent," I told her. "The guy's as pure as the driven snow, perhaps even purer. We're talking regular white knight material here. Chase Kingsley would never harm a woman or touch her in anger, nor force himself upon her. I'm pretty sure the commissioner and the Mayor's wife have both been very naughty, and did a real number on the poor fellow."

"No wonder he looks so angry all the time," she murmured, and I thought I could see a small smile tugging at her lips. My assessment of Chase had obviously pleased her, which just went to show I was right about them.

"So what do *you* think, Dooley?" she asked, keen to get a second opinion. Her dad is a doctor, after all, and we all know that doctors love to get second opinions—and third ones.

"Max is right," said Dooley. "Max is always right."

"That settles it," said Odelia, looking grim. "I'm going to expose the commissioner and the Mayor's wife and clear Chase's name."

I looked up in alarm. "Um, I wouldn't do that if I were you."

"Why not? He's been wrongfully accused. You said so yourself. It's my job to right this wrong. It's what I do."

Uh-oh. I shook my head. "If you're going after those two they'll simply deny the whole thing and get you fired. You'll never work in this town again."

"Ever, ever, ever again," said Dooley.

"They can't do that!" Odelia cried. "He doesn't have the authority. Dan would never fire me just because the NYPD commissioner says so."

"No, but they could make your life very difficult," I said. "These two are part of the happy few. They have powerful friends who might put the squeeze on Dan and his advertisers until he's forced to choose between you and his paper. No, if you're going after those two you'll have to do it the old-fashioned way: by launching a smear campaign."

"What do you mean?"

"You're a reporter. You write the story and credit an anonymous source." I pointed at myself and Dooley. "We're your anonymous sources."

"But how can I go after him? I don't have a shred of evidence."

"Leave that to us," I said. "First we'll find ourselves a witness of the commissioner's indiscretions, and then we'll get you your evidence. Like I said, someone somewhere saw those two, and, like with cats, nowadays smartphones are pretty much ubiquitous, so someone is bound to have snapped a picture, even if they didn't realize the significance of what they saw. And once those pictures surface, they'll corroborate the story you're about to write."

She smiled down at me. "You guys are really special, do you know that?"

"I do know that," I acknowledged.

"Just like Babe!" Dooley said happily.

"Just like Babe," I said. Dooley had been right all along. We were special.

CHAPTER 16

Odelia pulled the car up in front of the police station, and let the cats out. Dooley seemed reluctant to be shifted, so Max gave him a poke and he finally relented, muttering something about never being allowed to get any sleep.

"We have a job to do, Dooley," said Max solemnly. "Sleep can wait."

She watched the two cats stalk off, launching their all-important mission, and smiled to herself. If it hadn't been for her special talent of being able to talk to cats, her life would have looked quite different. She walked into the police station and waltzed straight past Dolores, who announced that the Chief was in, and would be happy to see her.

Happy or not, he was going to see her anyway. She needed to know what the medical examiner had discovered.

"Hey, Odelia," said her uncle when she breezed into his office. "I was just going to call you." And he held up his phone to prove he wasn't lying.

She plunked down in a chair and gave him a tense look. All this business with Chase had only served to take her

118

mind off the murder case, which was probably a whole lot more important than whether the detective was innocent of the crime he'd been accused of or not.

"Let's have it," she said. "How did Paulo Frey die?"

"Well," said her uncle, leaning back in his chair, "looks like good old-fashioned bludgeoning."

"Bludgeoning?"

"The guy had his head smashed in. And since we found a poker next to the body, that just might be our murder weapon. Especially since it was a little bent out of shape, exactly the shape of a person's head, actually."

She whistled through her teeth. "That must have been some hit."

"Yeah, whoever killed him hit him so hard they fractured his skull, which, according to the ME, is what caused his death. And a good thing, too."

"That's a little harsh. You didn't even know the guy."

Her uncle emitted a chuckle. "I mean that if he'd been stabbed or had his throat slit we might never have found out, as the body was too decomposed."

"Anything else? Chase told me you pinpointed the time of death?"

"Yeah, the techies discovered that Frey used to sync his smartphone to his laptop, which was an automated process, apparently. The last time he did was September sixteen, which is also the last time the laptop was accessed."

"Because it ended up in the cesspit along with the body."

"Exactly."

"Did you get anything off his phone?"

"Nope. We're checking his laptop, but so far it hasn't yielded any clues."

"No webcam picture of the killer bending over the victim while he was busy working on his next masterpiece?"

He laughed. "Now wouldn't that be something? But no. No picture of the killer."

"Too bad."

"Yeah." He gave her a quick look. "Chase tells me you keep popping up wherever he goes?"

"I could say the same thing about him."

"It's driving him nuts," said her uncle with a grin. "I guess NYPD cops aren't used to reporters interviewing suspects and going over the crime scene."

"I guess not," she said with a smile.

"You talked to Aissa Spring and Gabby Cleret, so there's not much you don't already know, I guess," he said, checking a file on his desk.

"Apart from the fact that Paulo Frey was not a nice person? I guess not."

"Yeah, he was a piece of work, all right," her uncle admitted. "I talked to Hetta Fried, by the way."

"The owner of the Writer's Lodge? What did she have to say?"

"Well, apparently Frey never paid his bills. He had this thing where he simply ignored any reminder she'd send him until she threatened with a lawsuit. Then he'd pay up, but only a fraction of the total amount."

"But why? I thought he was rich."

Her uncle shrugged. "Maybe that's how he got rich? He hadn't paid his bills for the last two years."

"And she still allowed him to come back?"

"Sure. Having a big-name author like him was good for business. Just the mention of his name on the website attracted a lot of lesser writers, who wanted to write in the same place as the master, hoping to catch some of that 'magic.'"

"I can't imagine Hetta would kill him over unpaid bills, though."

"Me neither. She wasn't going to kill the goose with the golden eggs, even if he didn't pay his bills. Besides, this murder is murder on her business. She told me she's received a dozen cancellations already and might have to close down the lodge if this keeps up."

"I guess lesser writers don't want to write where the master was killed."

"I guess not," he said with a grin. "Oh, and I also talked to the production company that went belly up after that Indiana Jones fracas."

She sat up. Now that was a valuable lead. "And? Any suspects?"

He studied his notes. "I talked to one of the principals, and he didn't have a lot of good things to say about Frey. In fact I don't think I've ever heard so many four-letter words in such a short space of time. But he also assured me he didn't kill Frey. And yes, I checked his alibi," he said before she could ask. "You're talking to an old dog here, honey. I know how to do my job. The guy was at a party in Beverly Hills, and so was his partner. So no dice."

"Too bad," she said, disappointed. That was such a good lead. Then she brightened. "Maybe they hired a professional to get rid of Frey?"

He stared at her. "Odelia, honey, movie producers don't go around having people killed. It's Hollywood, not the Mob."

She sank back down again. "Just saying it's a possibility."

"A very implausible one."

"So, um…" She stared at the desk. "Have you heard from Chase?"

He eyed her with a humorous expression on his face. "Yeah, he told me he saw you snooping around the lodge. He also told me you almost broke your neck."

"I didn't break my neck," she protested. "I would have

been perfectly fine if he hadn't started badgering me, causing me to lose my footing."

"So he caused you to lose your footing, huh? How did that happen?"

She noticed he was grinning from ear to ear, and so she glared at him. He was just as bad as Max and Dooley. Did everyone think she had a thing for Detective Kingsley now? "He caught me just as I was trying to get into the place."

"You should have asked for the key," he said, still smiling.

"I know, but it was one of those spur-of-the-moment decisions," she admitted. "I just thought I'd take a look."

"Well, you wouldn't have found anything of importance in there anyway. We searched that place top to bottom. Went over it with a crime scene team."

"No fingerprints?"

"Oh, sure. Lots and lots of them. That place gets rented out on a weekly basis, honey, and let me tell you, Rohanna Coral, whatever her other qualities, is a pretty reluctant cleaner. We found dust that hadn't been shifted in years."

"Yeah, I talked to Rohanna. She said Frey was a good tipper."

"At least someone got some money off the guy."

They stared at each other for a beat. "So who killed him?"

He shrugged. "I'm sure I don't know. And I'm also sure you'll find out."

She laughed. "And why is that?"

"You've got skills. Skills that no one else has. So…"

She studied him for a moment. She'd long suspected that her uncle knew about the special talent she'd inherited from his sister. Dad knew, of course. You can't live with three generations of women and not know. Had Marge told her brother? Or had he noticed her uncommon affinity with cats growing up together? She gave him a grateful smile. If he knew about their secret, he certainly hadn't told anyone. "Thanks, Uncle Alec."

He seemed taken aback. "What for?"

"For letting me be part of the investigation. And for your confidence."

He made a throwaway gesture. "Oh, nonsense. Anyone with a brain can see you're a natural at this stuff, honey."

"Chase Kingsley can't see it."

"Well," he said with a grin, "Chase is new. He's got a lot to learn about Hampton Cove and the way we do things around here. I'm sure that over time he'll start to see what a great addition you make to the team, in a non-official capacity. Now what are your plans? Where do we go from here?"

She chewed her lip for a moment. "You know, when I talked to Gabby, she mentioned something about there probably being other people out there that Frey must have slandered. How about I try to find those other victims? Maybe one of them finally snapped?"

"Great idea," he said. "Chase said something similar."

"Oh, Chase is looking into that angle too, huh?"

Uncle Alec scratched his scalp. "He's a great detective, actually." He eyed her wearily for a moment. "You may not see eye to eye with the guy, but he's a first-rate sleuth, and, just like you, a great addition to the team."

She nodded. "I know. It's just that he rubs me the wrong way, especially when he insists I'm just a nosy reporter and should mind my own business."

"Yeah, well, like I said, he'll get over that. I'm sure that's just a big-city kind of thing. Now that he's here in the sticks, he'll see we do things differently."

And with these wise words, he waved her off.

CHAPTER 17

Walking out of the police station, she wondered what her next course of action should be. How could she figure out who Frey's other victims were? And then she got it. All manner of vile abuse these days was done on social media. So where better to start her search than by going through Frey's feeds? If he'd targeted people, she was bound to find the evidence right there.

She headed back to the office and for the next couple of hours meticulously went through Frey's Facebook page, his Twitter feed and his Instagram. She even read his blog, and when she finally had enough, her view of Paulo Frey had taken a nosedive, if that was even possible.

The man was a troll, and not one of the nice cuddly ones with the brightly colored hair either, but a vicious, nasty one who stalked anyone he disagreed with. He'd engaged in online warfare with so many people it was a miracle he hadn't been killed sooner. Gabby Cleret was only the tip of the iceberg. Over the course of the last couple of years, he'd fought with so many people she wondered why people still bothered to read his books.

Surely readers must have discovered what a dreadful person he was by now?

But instead of abandoning him in droves, he'd actually garnered support for his trollish behavior. A group of rabid followers, calling themselves 'The Unafreyds,' admired his boldness and the way he dared say what others didn't, and had enthusiastically endorsed his attacks on reporters, actors, politicians and anyone else he didn't agree with. When he'd disagreed with a reporter for the *New York Times*, they'd actually gone after the man IRL, which was short for In Real Life, by picketing his house. He finally was forced to move to an undisclosed location with his wife and two kids.

Holy moly, she thought as she sat back. This guy was the worst of the worst. No wonder someone had taken a poker to the back of his head. The only question was who? Who of the dozens of people he'd harassed had finally taken matters into their own hands? It appeared there were a great number of candidates. All they needed to do was check them one by one, to see if they'd been in town that day.

She quickly compiled a list of the most egregious displays of online abuse, and emailed it to Uncle Alec. Then she rubbed her eyes and closed her laptop. Tonight she had that dinner with Chase Kingsley to look forward to, and if Max was right—and she had no doubt in her mind that he was—she owed the guy an apology. She wasn't going to offer him one, though, for his behavior against her didn't warrant one. She wasn't the commissioner and she hadn't gotten him fired from his job, so why he had to be so angry with her she didn't know. Sure, he had a bone to pick with the *New York Post*, but she didn't work for them. She was just a small-town reporter who had a modest newspaper to fill.

Which reminded her that the Paulo Frey case wasn't the only article that needed writing. So for the next couple of hours, she diligently typed up an article on the upcoming opening of a new flower shop on Bleecker Street, an article on the new Children's Room in the library—courtesy of her mother—and a small article on the mermaid festival that was taking place down at the marina. Anyone who wanted to compete had to show up in their best mermaid's costume and prove they could swim. The jury awarded a prize to the best one, and a picture would be featured on the front page of the paper.

Thinking of pictures... She quickly transferred the pictures she'd taken at the crime scene to her laptop, and leafed through them. She'd taken a couple of the pit, and suddenly got an idea. Uncle Alec said they'd gotten Frey's laptop to work but hadn't found any evidence on it so far. What if she could take a closer look at it? Now that she knew what kind of man Frey was, it stood to reason he'd been threatened over the years. What if he kept some of that stuff on his computer? Maybe it could provide a clue to the murderer?

She fired off another email to her uncle, asking him if she could take a look at the laptop, and he immediately wrote back to tell her she was more than welcome to have a peek, along with the other stuff they found in the pit.

Most of her work for the day done, she breezed into Dan's office.

"All done?" he asked, looking up from his computer.

"Yeah, pretty much," she said, leaning against the door. "I haven't solved the Frey murder. Yet. But the rest is done."

He laughed. "You're incredible, Odelia. You know," he said, removing his glasses and starting to polish them with the hem of his shirt, "I think you're going to solve this murder. I really do."

"Of course I'm going to solve this murder," she said with humorous bluster. "Who do you think I am? Some talentless hack?"

"No, you're definitely not a talentless hack," he agreed. "In fact I think hiring you was probably the best decision I ever made in a long career. Now shoo. I'll finish up here."

She grinned at the aged editor. "See you, Dan."

"See you, honey. Say hi to your folks for me."

"Will do."

As she climbed into her pickup, she took in the empty passenger seat, and wondered if Max and Dooley would have remembered the other story she'd been working on today: the secret affair of the NYPD commissioner and the Mayor's wife. And as she started up the car, she hoped they'd find proof of Chase's innocence. But even if they didn't, she knew they'd called it: the detective was innocent. She now realized she'd known all along, but had allowed her instincts to be clouded by her annoyance with the guy.

Chase might be a pain in the patootie, but he was not a molester of women.

She now wondered if maybe deep down she already knew who Frey's killer was. She thought for a moment. Somewhere at the back of her mind, the kernel of an idea was tugging, but she couldn't quite catch it. Something she'd missed. But what? And where? And more importantly, who?

CHAPTER 18

I think I'd been a little too optimistic when I told Odelia I'd solve this mystery in a heartbeat. Dooley and I had been traipsing all over town, talking to any cat we could find, and so far had nothing to show for our efforts. None of them had an inkling of who Chase Kingsley was, or the commissioner of the NYPD, or even the Mayor's wife for that matter, nor did they care.

Instead, they all shook their heads, convinced we'd both gone off our rockers. I should have known, of course. Cats, as you may or may not know, like to stick close to home. They like to wander around, preferably at night, when the world is asleep, in search of mice or other little snacks, but never stray far, for they like to be home before dawn, curl up at the foot of a warm, soft bed, and wait until their human wakes up to fill up their bowl of kibble.

We used to be proud hunters once upon a time, but centuries of being fed and nurtured by humans have made us lazy and complacent. New York is another continent, as far as we are concerned, and rarely do we even venture outside of Hampton Cove these days. Why should we, when all we need is right here at home?

Even my theory that we might run into a cat who'd met a cat who'd talked to a cat who'd caught the commissioner and the Mayor's wife in the act was pretty far-fetched, I now saw. Cats rarely travel. Dogs love to ride in cars, their heads sticking out of the window, their tongues lolling in the breeze, but then we all know that dogs are a little weird. Cats are dignified creatures. We wouldn't be seen dead with our tongues hanging out and our faces flapping in the wind.

And then there was the fact that both Dooley and I were bone-tired. Daytime is sleeping time, and we'd skipped nap time to go out hiking in the woods, and to play detective across town. It also explained why there weren't all that many cats around, and those that were, didn't want to be disturbed. The best time to do this was at night, Dooley reminded me as we dragged our weary bodies along the strip mall, on the edge of town.

"You're right," I admitted. "Let's call it quits and do this again tonight, when there are more cats around. Maybe we'll have better luck then."

"I kinda doubt it, Max," said Dooley. "Considering all the cats we talked to who have laughed in our faces, I think our chances of finding the one cat that saw the Mayor of New York having relations with the commissioner are slim."

"The Mayor's wife," I corrected him. "The Mayor's wife is having relations with the commissioner, not the Mayor."

"Oh, okay."

And we were just about to call it a day and return to our cozy home, when I happened to glance at a set of dumpsters located behind the mall and recognized a familiar figure snooping around in there.

"Don't look now, but I think I just saw Clarice," I whispered, even though she probably couldn't hear me from this distance.

"Clarice? Where?" Dooley asked, immediately starting to look around like a tourist on a tour bus.

"I said, don't look now," I hissed. "She's over there by those dumpsters."

I watched as the scrawny feline dove into one of the dumpsters, clearly fishing around for something edible.

"Poor creature," Dooley said ruefully. "No home, no warm bed, and no food."

"I don't know," I said. "Maybe it's not so bad. At least she gets to choose her food. I'll bet there's some choice stuff in those dumpsters."

"I see what you mean. Do you think there's raw meat in there?"

"Raw meat, pizza, lasagna, a nice beef burger. You name it, they got it."

"Maybe we'll have a peek?" he suggested. "I wouldn't mind having a nibble at some raw meat."

"What's with this sudden raw meat obsession?"

He shrugged. "I can't help it that Brutus gets fed raw meat and I don't, can I? And that because of that he's better looking and more attractive to certain female felines."

"Actually, I'm not so sure about that," I intimated.

"What do you mean?"

"What if he's lying? He wouldn't be the first cat to turn out to be a liar."

"You mean he's lying about the meat?"

"Why not? There's no way for us to check."

"He's messing with us! And deceiving poor Harriet."

"Don't feel sorry for Harriet. If she chooses that brute it's her funeral."

"Funeral!" he cried, his voice skipping an octave. "Do you really believe that horrible creep would hurt her?"

"It's just an expression," I said. "Let's have a chat, shall we?" And I started tripping over to the dumpsters.

"A chat?" he asked, falling into step beside me. "With who?"

"With whom," I corrected him. We might be cats, but that was no excuse for a lapse in grammar. "Who do you think?"

"Is this a trick question? Don't do this to me, Max. Not when I'm tired. Just tell me already. Whommmm are we going to chat with?"

"Clarice, of course."

He gulped. "Clarice? She'll just tell us she saw nothing."

"Well, maybe she will, and maybe she won't. But it's definitely worth a try."

Of all the cats I know in Hampton Cove, Clarice is the one who has traveled the most and traveled the farthest. She has to, to find food and shelter, as she doesn't have a human to take care of her. Once upon a time, the rumor went, she did have a human, but they'd abandoned her. Some tourist who came to Hampton Cove for the holidays, tied her to a tree and took off. The same rumor held that she had actually gnawed off her own paw to escape, though from what I'd seen all of her limbs were still present and accounted for, so that story might have been a fabrication.

"Clarice," I called out as we approached the dumpster she was currently holed up in. "Clarice, we'd like to talk to you." The small collection of dumpsters was where the stores the mall was comprised of dumped their garbage, and was always a place where all manner of critters gathered.

When Clarice popped up out of the dumpster, shifty-eyed and ready to flee, Dooley chimed in, "Hey, Clarice. So we meet again, huh? What are the odds?" He looked a little afraid, and with good reason. Clarice has been known to lash out when she is approached without invitation.

"We were just wondering—" I began.

"I know nothing," she said, repeating her usual mantra.

"Yeah, yeah, yeah," I said, a little gruffly. I wasn't in the mood for games. I was tired and hungry and my paws hurt. "Look, all we need to know is whether you know a cat who knows a cat who might have seen a cat who…"

"I know nothing," Clarice repeated.

"See? I told you this was a waste of time," said Dooley. He'd planted himself on his rear end and was sniffing the air, probably looking for meat.

"Look, we just want to know—"

"I know nothing!" she repeated, and jumped out of the dumpster, giving us both the dirtiest of looks and starting to walk away.

"Now hold it right there!" I cried. "All we want is information. Is that too much to ask? If you tell us what we need to know we'll even share our kibble with you next time you're in the neighborhood. Isn't that right, Dooley?"

Dooley stared at me. He obviously didn't agree. If anyone was going to share their kibble, it was going to be me. Well, that was fine. From experience I knew that fresh kibble was only a trip to the store away.

I gulped a little, because Clarice was giving me her best stare. So now I was locked in a stare-down with the most feral cat in Hampton Cove. If she lashed out and scratched my nose, that would set the seal on this day. To my surprise, she didn't. Instead, she said, "Oh, all right, Max, you annoying little weasel. What do you want to know?"

Relieved, I told her about the murder of Paulo Frey. It turned out that the Writer's Lodge was like a second home to her. Which, now that I thought about it, wasn't surprising. Writers are an easy mark for a cat's affections, as a lot of them genuinely like us. Most of them got cats at home, and when they come out to the woods to write they miss their little furballs. So when they see Clarice lurking in the woods, they try to lure her by offering her the best treats. I now saw what her MO was, and with it came a newfound respect.

"Well, I don't know anything about that Chase Kingsley affair," she finally said, "and I don't really care. What humans do is none of my business. What I can tell you is I saw someone drag the body of that writer out of the lodge a year ago, so I'm guessing that might have been your killer."

Dooley and I exchanged excited glances. "You saw the killer?" I asked.

"Sure, sure," she said, studying her nails, which were razor-sharp. "They dragged the body of that Frey guy out of the lodge and dumped it where they like to do their business. Made a nice big splash, too. Then they came out again and dumped a bunch of other stuff in there."

"A laptop and a couple of suitcases," I said.

"Sure, sure," she said, rolling her eyes, already bored with the conversation.

"So?" I asked when she was silent for a beat. "Who was it?!"

"Yeah, Clarice," Dooley huffed out. "Who's the killer?"

"What's it worth to you?" she asked, removing a fishbone from between her teeth and giving it a tentative nibble.

"Whatever you want," I said excitedly.

"I'll take a twenty-pound bag of fish kibble. The expensive stuff. And a couple bags of that party mix you guys seem to like so much. Mixed grill."

"Deal!" I cried.

Clarice gave a chuckle, spit out the fishbone and suddenly, fast as lightning, flicked a paw beneath the dumpster and came away with a sizable rat, dragging it out by its tail. And then, before our horrified gaze, she gobbled down the rat, hide and hair!

I gulped and so did Dooley. We weren't necessarily rat hunters, what with having such a cushy life and all, and watching this… massacre taking place in front of our eyes reminded us we were as far removed from our feral ancestors as felinely possible.

"So, those are my terms," Clarice said, spitting out the rat tail and using it to pick her teeth. "I want the best stuff. Take it or leave it."

"Sure! Fine! All right!" I cried. "I can get you all of that and more."

I was pretty sure that Odelia wouldn't mind trading a couple of expensive bags of cat food for the identity of Paulo Frey's killer. It was a bargain!

Clarice held up her paw, then sliced it with the nail of her other paw. A small drop of blood dribbled down. I thought I was going to faint at the sight of the blood, and it was obvious Dooley was feeling the same way.

"Put it there, fellas," she said in that gravelly voice of hers. "Let's seal the deal with blood."

"Is that really necessary?" asked Dooley in a choked voice.

"No blood, no deal," growled Clarice.

"What is this, the Middle Ages?" squeaked Dooley. "I thought we were past all this nonsense."

"All right, all right," I said, fearing Clarice would change her mind. So I held up my left paw and made a small incision. A drop of blood appeared, and I suddenly felt queasy. That's the curse of being a house cat: you lose those killer instincts.

"Now you, Dooley," I said.

"Yeah. Now you, Dooley," said Clarice in a mocking voice. "Put it there, pal." She was simply taunting us, I realized. Playing with us, as if we were mice. Or rats.

"I can't," he cried. "I can't stand the sight of blood. And I— I hate the pain!" he added with a pathetic whiny voice.

"Oh, for crying out loud," Clarice grunted. "What are you, a cat or a mouse? Come here, you pansy-ass puss." And with a vicious slicing movement, she scratched Dooley's nose.

"Owowowowow!" he cried. "What did you do that for?!"

"Because you're a whiny little pussy," she said, and put her hand up to his nose, giving it a hearty pat. "Now you, Max. Slap one on this sissy's nose."

I put my paw against hers and Dooley's nose, so that our blood mingled. It was a very unhygienic affair, I thought, and as I did it, I winced. Dooley mewled a little, and obviously didn't like his nose squeezed between my paw and Clarice's. He bore it bravely, though, probably because he didn't have a choice. If he ran for the hills now, Clarice would probably hunt him down and eat him alive, just like she'd gobbled up that rat!

Clarice finally grunted her approval. "It's not your regular blood oath," she said as she gave Dooley a nasty glare, "but I guess it'll do."

And, as promised, she proceeded to put us on the scene she'd witnessed over a year ago, when Paulo Frey had lost his life. Both Dooley and I gasped when we finally learned the identity of the killer, and stared at each other in abject horror. All this time I'd figured that some outsider had done the terrible deed, and not one of our own, but now it turned out that evil had been much closer than we'd imagined. We'd nursed a viper at our bosoms, and Hampton Cove would never be the same again after this startling revelation.

"I'll come and collect one of these days," Clarice reminded me, and then seemed to take pity on us. "Cheer up, fellas," she snarled. "It's a tough world out there. Kill or be killed. No need to get all mushy on me. You're proud cats, for crying out loud, not a couple of lily-livered puppies. Learn to love the pain! Love it!"

After dispensing these pearls of wisdom, she trotted off, leaving bloody paw prints behind. Long after she'd left,

Dooley and I still sat there, staring into space, Dooley with blood dripping down his nose, which he occasionally gave a lick, and me holding up my paw and also licking it in a steady rhythm. I wasn't going to go walkabout now, not with that cut. It just might infect and cause gangrene and then my entire leg would have to come off, and how would I look then? I know, I know. Dooley and I are not exactly feral. We're house cats, used to the good life. Used to being pampered and spoiled. At least we'd just solved the Paulo Frey murder.

After what seemed like the longest time, we set a course for the homestead, and Dooley was the first one to break the silence.

"Who would have thought?"

"Yeah, who would have thunk?"

We didn't speak again. We were both bone-tired, and the moment we arrived home, we both dropped our weary bodies down, me on my favorite spot on the couch, and Dooley right next to me. He'd asked to crash at our place, as he didn't want to risk coming across Harriet and Brutus, and I'd magnanimously agreed. Dooley and I are like brothers, and my space is his space. Besides, we'd just made a blood oath, so now we were blood brothers.

And then we both fell into a deep, healing sleep, dreaming of cruel killers and feral cats and big bags of the best kibble Odelia's money could buy.

CHAPTER 19

Odelia parked the pickup across the street from the library. It was located on its own patch of land, and fronted by a small garden that sported several flower beds and looked as colorful, cozy and inviting as the library itself, the place where her mother Marge had worked all her life. A neo-Elizabethan style building, it looked like something transported from England and plunked down there in their pleasant little town. Once inside, it got even better, as high ceilings and open spaces invited you in. Hampton Covians young and old gathered there to find their favorite book or to listen to one of the writers occasionally asked to read from their work.

Recently the library had been expanded with a children's section, which was the pride and talk of the town. Odelia didn't have to look long for her mother, who was at the desk, checking out a couple of books for a young mother and her two kids. While she waited until her mom was free, Odelia strode to the newspaper and magazine nook and took a seat. A copy of her very own *Hampton Cove Gazette* was on display, right next to big boys like the *New York Times*, the *Washington*

Post and *USA Today*. Of course the local press was also represented: *Dan's Papers* and the *East Hampton Star* had pride of place.

She picked up a copy of *Time Magazine* and saw that it featured an article on Paulo Frey, on the occasion of his disappearance one year ago. She leafed through the article, and saw that the reporter, like most people, simply assumed the writer had gone off to write a novel somewhere on an exotic island, and would soon return clutching a voluminous tome that would prove his enduring masterpiece. Little did they know he'd been resting at the bottom of a pit all this time.

She placed the magazine back on the stand and wandered over to the new children's section, past rows and rows of neatly indexed books. The children's room sported a large boat, where kids could sit and read, and other creative nooks as well, all in a bid to inspire the new generation to take up the habit of picking up a book from time to time. In this day and age of electronic devices, it was sometimes hard to get kids to read, when they could watch a cartoon on their tablet or phone instead, and the new wing had been designed to provide kids with a sense of curiosity about the world of books, and to instill them with a love for the medium that would hopefully last a lifetime.

"Great space, huh?" her mother asked when she joined her. Marge Poole was a fine-boned woman with long blond hair, just like her daughter, and soft, brown eyes that spoke of her humanity. She was soft-spoken and sweet-tempered, and had been a mainstay at the library for the past twenty years.

She now stepped into the boat and picked up a picture book of Jonah and the Whale and started flipping its pages. Odelia joined her and picked up a Garfield comic book. Garfield always reminded her of Max.

"So how are things at the paper?" Marge asked.

"Great," said Odelia. The boat was even more spacious than she'd imagined, even for two grown-ups, so she gathered for kids it was enormous. "I'm working on an article about the Paulo Frey murder case."

"I heard about that," said her mother, looking up. "What a horrible thing to happen in Hampton Cove. Who would have thought something like that was even possible? It's more something you'd expect in New York, not here."

"Yeah, it's not something that happens every day," she agreed, then decided to broach a topic that might lead her into trouble. "Dad told me you invited that new cop for dinner? Chase Kingsley?"

Her mother's face lit up with a smile. "Such a nice young man. I figured since he's new in town, it would be a good idea to offer him a home-cooked meal and show him that Hampton Cove is a genuinely hospitable town."

"So you met him?"

"Alec brought him by the library to introduce him."

"He, um…" She hesitated. "Did he tell you about his previous career?"

"Alec told me Chase used to work for the NYPD."

"Did he also tell you how he got fired?"

Her mom's eyes widened. "Fired? No, he didn't tell me about that."

In a few brief words she explained why it was that Hampton Cove had suddenly gained a policeman while the NYPD had lost one. She also added that Max and Dooley were convinced that the man was innocent of the charges, and that they'd set out to prove it.

"Of course he's innocent," said her mother now. "A man like that could never be guilty of such a heinous crime. Molestation, no less. I think I would recognize a molester when I saw one, and Chase definitely isn't one. In fact I'm

139

surprised you thought for a moment he could be guilty of such a crime."

She shrugged. "Like I told Dad, we got off on the wrong foot. He took a dislike to me, simply because I'm a reporter, and then things escalated."

"We'll settle all of that tonight. You and Chase can take a stroll after dinner and work things out. Kiss and make up," she said blithely.

Odelia blinked, and felt her cheeks redden. "Um, I don't know about that," she said. "He seems to hate my guts, especially after…"

Her mother frowned. "After what?"

"Nothing," she muttered, idly toying with a particularly colorful troll that was placed on the edge of the boat. Which reminded her… "Did you know that Frey had a reputation for trolling people? Especially women of size?"

"No, I didn't," said her mother, surprised. "Are you sure?"

"Pretty much. He trolled Gabby Cleret and Marissa Dixon and a lot of others. Turns out he wasn't such a nice person, and whoever killed him was probably one of his victims."

"I can't imagine. He was in here often, you know."

This surprised her. "He was?"

"Well, as a writer of his stature we took every opportunity to invite him for readings. He was extremely accommodating and always proved a big hit."

She gave her mother a grin. "So you can't recognize a molester of women after all, huh?"

Marge pursed her lips in disapproval. "Are you sure those aren't just rumors and gossip? Paulo Frey never struck me as an unpleasant man. Quite the contrary. I thought he was extremely charming, and eager to please."

"Yes, I'm sure, Mom," she said, remembering Marissa's story, and Gabby's harrowing tale. "He was not a nice man."

"Well, I'm sure you're right," said her mother, fiddling with a troll. They were placed throughout the library because of a special screening of the movie *Trolls*. "I just hope they catch his killer soon. I'd hate for anyone else to get hurt."

"I don't think anyone else is going to get hurt. This was personal."

"Well, I'm sure Alec and Chase will capture the killer soon enough."

"Not if I catch him first."

This elicited a frown from her mother. "Honey, you're not a detective. You're a reporter. Why don't you leave this nasty business to your uncle?"

"Because I have an instinct for solving crime, Mom, even Uncle Alec said so."

"Yes, but that doesn't mean you have to go and willingly put yourself in harm's way. Messing around with murder is extremely dangerous."

"I'm sure that this killer only ever intended to make one victim," she said, brushing off her mother's concerns. Mom was always worried about her safety. She'd been even more worried when she'd been away in New York, in college, and only came home on the weekends. Now that she was home again, living next door, she still worried. Even though she was proud that her little girl was a reporter, she'd much rather have seen her pursue a career fraught with less danger. Like a doctor, following in her father's footsteps.

In her mother's hopes and dreams for her future, she'd always seen her work alongside her father, so she could take over when he retired one day. Even her father had faintly harbored that wish. But she'd never had any interest in the medical profession. Journalism had been her first love, and she'd always known that when she grew up she'd be a reporter, just like Dan. Even though she'd had loftier ambitions at the time. She'd wanted to be a reporter for one of the big papers. Or even one of the big networks. But she'd soon discovered that at heart she was a small-town girl, and had to accept she'd never make a career anywhere else. She'd never fly overseas to cover a war, or interview the leaders of the world gathered in Davos. And she was fine with that. She was happy right here in Hampton Cove, covering the opening of a new library wing, or the mermaid festival.

"Look, this is what I do, Mom," she said. "And I'm sure that whoever this killer is, they aren't going to come after me."

"How can you be so sure?" asked her mother, worry etched on her features.

"Call it a hunch. This killer isn't a serial killer. It's someone pushed too far by Frey. Someone who decided enough was enough. Whoever this is, isn't going to kill again, I'm sure of it."

"Unless you get too close," said her mother, looking fearful. "And then they will lash out, simply to keep you from discovering the truth."

"That's not going to happen. You know me. I'm always very careful."

"I wish you'd just leave all this business to your uncle Alec and this nice young policeman. They can take care of themselves. That's what they're trained for."

She saw she would never be able to convince her mother, so she decided to change the subject. "Any idea how to convince Hampton Cove that Chase is innocent of the crime he's been accused of?"

Her mother frowned at this. "Convince? Why, there's nothing to convince. Anyone can see he's a perfectly nice young man with impeccable morals."

"Not everyone is as welcoming and perceptive as you, Mom."

She would have used the word 'naive,' but that was a little harsh.

"I'm sure that once they get to know Chase, those rumors will go away."

"I very much doubt it."

"Well, I don't," Mom said breezily as she got out of the boat. A library visitor had caroled out a loud 'Yoo-hoo!'

Odelia didn't share her mother's optimism. She thought that the moment the story hit the town about Chase's dismissal, they'd petition the Mayor to have him fired. And if enough people signed that petition, the Mayor and Uncle Alec would have no choice but to let him go. Even though until a couple of hours ago she'd believed herself that he was a bad person, she now saw that a gross miscarriage of justice had been carried out, and that if it wasn't rectified, this business would haunt him for the rest of his life. And even though the man was as stubborn and pigheaded as anyone she'd ever known, he didn't deserve that.

With a sigh, she got up and climbed out of the boat. A little girl had run up and was eyeing her a little timidly. Adults usually didn't go and sit in the children's boat. She gave the girl a sweet smile and handed her the troll she'd been holding. "The boat is all yours, honey," she said. "Knock yourself out."

She watched how the girl and her sister hopped into the boat and started playing with the trolls, then picked up a book and started reading. She smiled, wondering if one day her own kids would be sitting there, with her watching on. She firmly put the thought out of her mind. Until she met the right guy, that wasn't a prospect she liked to dwell on.

She returned to the front of the library, and was greeted by Gran, who'd been rummaging around between the bookshelves, replacing returned books. She used a small cart to do it, which was now empty. For the occasion she was wearing a long, black coat, claiming there was a draft in the library, and she needed to protect herself. With her little white curls peeping from beneath a lime-green knit cap she'd placed on her head, she looked like an eighties punk rocker.

"So? Did you catch that killer?" asked Gran.

"Not yet, but I'm getting closer."

"You better catch him soon. This place ain't safe with that monster on the loose."

"I'm sure he or she isn't going to attack anyone else, Gran," she promised.

"How would you know? You're not a killer," snapped her grandmother. "They might very well be prowling the streets as we speak, looking for their next victim." She shivered. "I wouldn't like to cross paths with that beast."

"You won't," she said.

Gran glanced at a late visitor who was still browsing. She was the mother of the two girls now happily ensconced in the children's boat.

"I wish they wouldn't come in five minutes before closing time," Gran grumbled. "Don't they know we've got more important things to do?"

"Like what? Playing Scrabble with Dad?"

Lately, Gran and Dad had discovered a mutual fondness for Scrabble. Gran might bitch and moan about Dad, claiming he worked her like a dog, but secretly she liked her son-in-law. She now spent her mornings helping him out by picking up the phone and guiding traffic in the waiting room, and in the afternoon helped out Mom at the library while Dad was on his own.

"I like Scrabble," she said. "Sue me."

"I think you like Dad," she teased. "And Scrabble is just an excuse to spend more time with him."

"As if!" cried the old lady. "I'm doing him a favor. My time is precious, and I'm a regular saint for devoting so much of it to your dad." The customer dropped a book and Gran jumped. "Jeez! Wanna give me a heart attack?"

It was obvious this whole murder business had rattled her. "You know this killer will never harm you, right, Gran?" she asked.

"Tell that to the coroner when they haul my body from a cesspit."

She laughed. "That will never happen."

Gran glared at her. "Oh? How are you so sure?"

She shrugged. "I just know."

"Been talking with Max again, have you? Did that cat give you a clue?"

"Not yet, but he's out there, trying to figure out what happened."

"Leave it to the cats to solve this crime," she grunted. "They're a darn lot more capable than that worthless uncle of yours."

For some reason, Gran had never been convinced of Uncle Alec's crime-solving capabilities, and she didn't mind reminding him of that. She'd always hoped her son would go into politics and become the next mayor of Hampton Cove. That way she could brag to her friends. In her eyes, being a cop was nothing to brag about.

"I'm sure Uncle Alec is very capable," Odelia said, taking up her uncle's defense.

"And I'm sure he's not. Or that beefcake he's hired to do his dirty work."

"Beefcake? You mean Chase Kingsley?"

"I don't know what he's called. I just call him Captain Beefcake, on account of the fact that the looks like one of them male models you always see prancing around on the beach."

The image of Chase prancing around on the beach suddenly flashed before her mind's eye. She was sure from what she'd seen that the man was all lean muscle, and the image wasn't one she wanted in her head right now.

Gran eyed her closely. "You're sweet on the guy, aren't you? Figures."

"No, I'm not!"

But Gran wagged a finger in her face. "Let me give you a piece of advice, missy: Captain Beefcake is trouble with a capital T. Take it from one who knows about these things."

Gran just might be right for a change, she thought ruefully. If those strange jitters in her belly were anything to go by, she was in big trouble.

CHAPTER 20

*D*inner was served exactly at seven, with the entire Poole clan pitching in. Before dinner, Odelia had slipped over to her place to freshen up a little, and saw that the two cats lay passed out on the couch. They didn't even stir when she breezed past and then hurried out again. In fact they looked completely bushed, and it wasn't hard to see why. Usually they slept during the day and spent all night out and about. Today they'd snooped around all day, and were exhausted. She gave them a gentle stroke, and then left with a smile. She'd talk to them tonight, and see if they'd been able to come up with anything.

She'd opted for linen pants and a black blouse, applying minimal makeup. She refused to go all out, not wanting Detective Kingsley to think she was dressing up for his sake. She didn't want to reward the man's arrogance.

They'd prepared a simple meal of meatloaf, mashed potatoes and veggies, with a side salad, and when their guests finally arrived, the table was set. Before dinner, aperitifs were in order, as Odelia's dad—and Gran— liked their preprandial drink. When the doorbell rang, and Mom went to open the door, drinks were served even before Uncle Alec and Chase walked in.

Alec, who knew his way around his sister's place, accepted a martini from Dad, who then offered one to Chase, who politely declined.

Odelia, looking on from the kitchen entrance, couldn't help but notice that the detective looked even more handsome than that afternoon. He'd put on a crisply fresh white cotton shirt, snugly fitting jeans low on narrow hips, and his dark brown hair curled across his brow in a sexy sweep. The man could have been an advertisement for a brand of jeans, or an advertisement for whatever. With a muscular frame like that, she'd definitely buy whatever he was selling, and she was pretty sure other women would feel the same way.

Speaking of other women, it didn't escape her attention that the moment Chase walked into the living room, both Mom and Gran lavished their attention on him. Shaking her head, she picked up her own drink—flat water—and joined her dad and uncle out on the porch. They were already engaged in conversation about the murder case, with Uncle Alec discussing some of the medical aspects of the case, and Dad providing his professional opinion.

Out in the backyard, she saw Harriet languidly enjoying the lowering sun rays, licking her snowy white fur, while a new cat she'd never seen before looked on. The newcomer was black as night and looked gorgeous. This, she assumed, was the famous Brutus, and the reason Max and Dooley were in such a tizzy. She could see why. A prime specimen like this walking into their lives and stealing the attention of the only female in their small band of three was bound to upset the delicate balance that had existed all of their lives.

"Black and white. Nice combo," a sonorous voice spoke behind her. She knew Chase was referring to the cats, but he might as well have been talking about them, with her black blouse and his white shirt.

She squinted at the cats, who only had eyes for each other. "Is it just me but does that big, black cat look like it's about to pounce on poor Harriet?"

"From where I'm standing it looks like he's trying to figure out what makes her tick," Chase said. Turning, she noticed he was clutching a drink, something amber in a tumbler. So either Gran or Mom must have persuaded him to adhere to the Poole house rules and accept an aperitif after all.

"Oh?" she asked. "So he doesn't strike you as a lecherous creep?"

He grinned and took a sip from his drink. "Nope. He strikes me as a cat who's in way over his head, and doesn't know what he's gotten himself into."

Now it was her turn to smile. "That's what you get when you transport a big-city cat to a small town. They tend to underestimate the locals."

"Yeah, you just might be right about that," he grunted. "Though the same can be said about the locals. They tend to completely misjudge newcomers. Assign them all kinds of qualities they don't even remotely possess."

"And what qualities might that be?" she asked sweetly. "Arrogance? Pigheadedness? Refusal to accept the status quo?"

"You seem to forget that the newcomer has a distinct advantage."

"And what's that?"

"The advantage of the outside view. A fresh set of eyes on a situation that may look all too familiar to those who grew up in this town, and might miss the obvious staring them in the face."

She looked up sharply. "Why do I get the impression we're not talking about that nasty cat of yours?"

"Nasty?" he asked with a chuckle. "There's nothing nasty about Brutus."

"He's been terrorizing my cats," she said. "Muscling in on their territory and—" She gestured at Harriet "—persecuting their poor, helpless friend."

"That Persian doesn't strike me as helpless," he said. "On the contrary, she seems to enjoy the attention. In fact she downright revels in it."

"I think she's simply intimidated. She probably can't wait to get away from the brute but is scared he might become aggressive if she makes a move."

Now it was his turn to frown. "I'll have you know that Brutus has never in his life needed to resort to strong-arm tactics to get a female's attention."

"Well, he's not in the big city now, is he? He's in Hampton Cove, where cats are different and might not respond to him the way he's used to."

He laughed. "You're darn right about that. This place is like nothing I've ever seen. For one thing, in New York, reporters don't investigate crime."

"Well, out here they do, so you better get used to it, Detective."

"Yeah, I can see that," he said, scratching the back of his head sheepishly.

She stared at him in surprise. Was he finally seeing things her way?

"Have you interviewed any more suspects?" she asked.

"If I had I wouldn't tell you," he said simply.

So much for seeing things her way. "I thought as much. Good thing Uncle Alec keeps me informed, otherwise I'd never be able to catch this killer."

"Now look here, Miss Poole…"

"No, you look here, Detective. I'm going to catch this killer before you even sniff out your first clue. *That's* the way we do things down here."

"And I'll have you know, Miss Poole, that you're in way over your head. Catching killers is police business, and reporters like you should stick to what they're good at: writing about mermaids and children's library wings."

In spite of herself she had to smile at that. Dan must have posted her articles on the site after she left. "So you've been reading my stuff?"

"I have," he admitted. "I need to soak in the atmosphere so I had to start somewhere. Alec suggested I start with the *Gazette* and take it from there."

"You forgot about the opening of the new flower shop on Bleecker Street," she said with a grin. "Possibly some of my best writing to date."

"You are a great writer," he admitted. "Which is why you should stick to that, and make sure you keep out of harm's way."

"Is that concern I detect in your voice, Detective?" she asked.

"Of course. We're dealing with a killer here, who might not like it when you get too close."

"So you're admitting I'm getting close to solving this case?"

"I'm admitting that you're not trained to deal with a murderer on the loose, and I'd feel a lot better if you would leave the sleuthing to your uncle and myself."

They were at a standoff, and stood staring at each other, tension rising. But then Gran stepped in, holding up a tray of hors d'oeuvres and offering one to Chase. "Hors d'oeuvre, Detective Kingsley? I made them myself."

He finally broke eye contact. "Thanks," he said, popping one into his mouth.

"Has Odelia been bothering you, Detective?" Gran asked, darting a censorious glance at her granddaughter.

"She's been making a case for inserting herself into my investigation."

"Oh, she keeps doing that," said Gran, clucking her tongue. "She keeps inserting herself where she shouldn't. That's the nosy reporter type for you."

"Gran," said Odelia warningly. If even her own flesh and blood was turning against her, how could she ever hope to best this overbearing cop?

"What?" asked Gran innocently. "I was just apprising Detective Kingsley of all the facts pertaining to the case. If he's going to live and work in this town, it's important he gets the lay of the land."

"And I, for one, am mighty grateful for that, Mrs…"

"Muffin. Vesta Muffin," said Gran. "I'm a widow, you know, so if you invited me over for dinner, nobody in town would talk." She twiddled her ring-free hand in front of Chase, frivolously batting her eyes. "Free as a bird," she said with a sound that was probably supposed to be a seductive purr but came out like a lascivious growl.

Oh God, Odelia thought. If Gran was going to throw herself at Chase, the cop's opinion of her family would sink even lower.

"Thanks for the offer, Mrs. Muffin," said Chase. "That's very kind of you." He was looking slightly bewildered at this unexpected approach, but Odelia wasn't liking him well enough to come to his aid. If he thought he could handle killers and murderers so much better than she could he would have no trouble handling a septuagenarian with an overactive libido.

Which reminded her of something. She gestured at the two cats out in the yard. "Is that cat of yours fixed, Detective?"

"Why do you ask?" he asked, visibly glad for the change of topic.

"Because it's the law. Cats are supposed to be spayed or neutered."

"Are you afraid Brutus might sow his wild oats?" he quipped with a twinkle in his eye.

"I don't care about his oats. I'm simply concerned that our new law officer is already breaking the law, so soon after arriving in town."

"Of course Brutus is fixed," said Chase with a shrug. "So your precious Persian has nothing to worry about."

"Actually she's *my* precious Persian," said Mom, joining them. She was carrying another tray. "Finger food, Detective Kingsley? I made it myself."

"Thank you, Mrs. Poole."

"Marge, please."

"You've got a lovely home here, Marge. And a great family," he added with an appreciative nod at Odelia and Gran. Faced with three generations of women, it was obvious the cop was enjoying the attention, and the food, though he kept eyeing Gran a little warily as she sidled up to him.

"I like your guns," she said, licking her lips.

"My... guns?" said Chase, automatically reaching for his absent holster.

"Do you work out a lot?" she continued, making her point clear.

"Oh, those guns," he said. "Um, yeah, I like to hit the gym a couple times a week. Matter of trying to stay in shape in case I need to chase a bad guy."

"I can see how that might be important for a cop," Gran said, and made a tentative gesture in the direction of Chase's bicep, but restrained herself at the last moment. "Are you a meat-eater, Chase?"

"Yes, ma'am, as a matter of fact I am. Why, is this a vegan household?"

"No, of course not," said Mom. "Just the idea. Though Odelia went through a vegan episode, didn't you, honey?"

"Ever since she broke up with that no-good loser Sam Scurf."

"My eating habits got nothing to do with Sam," said Odelia, mortified. She so didn't want to discuss her dating life—or the lack thereof—in front of Chase.

"Who's this Sam?" asked Chase interestedly.

"He was a crook and a loser," Gran eagerly supplied. "She even brought him home once, and next thing we knew he'd embezzled half a million dollars from the Armstrong & Tillich Bank. They caught him, though, and threw his ass in the slammer. But then Odelia always had lousy taste in men." She glared at her grandmother, but the old lady ignored her. "She once dated a cop, you know. Appalachian. Until Alec discovered he was wanted in a dozen states and had supplied false credentials." She shook her snowy white head. "Always dating the bad guys, our poor Odelia."

Odelia raised her eyes to the heavens, praying that Gran would lay off already, but the stories seemed to amuse and entertain, for Chase asked, "Any other known criminals she dated?"

"Oh, plenty, but if I told you I'd have to kill you," Gran said with a grin, and then she did attach herself to Chase's arm and gave his bicep a squeeze. "Oh, my. How much did you say you curled, Chase?"

"I, um…"

Even Mom now seemed to notice the warning signs, for she swept in and took Gran into the house. "Let's freshen up a little before dinner, shall we?"

"I don't need freshening up," Gran sputtered. "I'm fresh as a daisy."

Chase seemed relieved at the removal of his stalker, and nodded at the house where the two women disappeared inside. "She's a feisty one, that grandmother of yours."

"Feisty and horny," said Odelia before she could stop herself. She slapped a hand in front of her mouth, mortified. "I'm sorry. That came out wrong."

Chase laughed, and she watched as twin dimples appeared on his cheeks. They made the already outrageously handsome cop look even more irresistible, and she admonished herself that after dating all the 'bad guys' of her past, like Gran had indicated, she didn't need to add another one to the list. The others might all have turned out to be crooks, but she had the distinct impression Chase Kingsley might give them a run for their money.

"Dinner is served!" Mom called out at that moment, and just in time, too, for Odelia had run out of things to say without making a total and utter fool of herself. Dinner at the Pooles had always been a demonstration in humiliation for her when there were men around, and tonight proved no exception. She just hoped they'd make it through dinner without Gran throwing herself at Chase, or providing a play-by-play of her granddaughter's disastrous dating life.

CHAPTER 21

*C*hase didn't stay after dinner, no matter how much Gran would have wanted him to. He claimed he still had work to do, and Odelia wondered if he was referring to the Frey case. She'd wanted to pick his brain, but it was obvious he wasn't going to allow her to do so. She tried to turn the conversation to the murder, but Chase brushed off all her attempts, much to Uncle Alec's amusement, who'd taken his new protégé's cue and also decided to keep this dinner Frey-free. Usually he enjoyed discussing ongoing cases over dinner, but apparently tonight he'd decided not to talk shop.

Odelia just hoped this wouldn't be the new normal, or else she'd have a lot less stuff to write about in the paper.

Chase quickly excused himself, and when Uncle Alec and Dad settled themselves on the couch to watch a football game, she suddenly felt an uncharacteristic fatigue sweep over her. All this trudging around had made her long for a good night's sleep, and after washing the dishes with Mom and Gran, who both couldn't get enough of gabbing about Chase, she bade her family goodnight and returned home.

She checked on Max and Dooley, but they were still passed out, and she decided not to disturb them. Tomorrow was another day, and they could resume their sleuthing efforts with renewed vigor. She was out like a light before her head even hit the pillow and may or may not have dreamed of handsome hunky cops warding off nosy reporters from their investigation.

The next morning, she drove to the office and parked her car. After checking her emails, she decided to walk down to the police station. She needed to check that laptop, to see if there were any clues to other enemies Frey might have made. When she arrived, she was surprised to find Chase already there. He was seated in front of Frey's laptop, intently staring at the screen, his hulking frame dwarfing one of the chairs in the evidence room. The rest of the evidence was spread out across the table, and when she walked in Chase didn't look up. Instead, he growled, "Morning, Miss Poole."

"How did you even know I was coming in?" she asked, her eye falling on the poker that indeed had a slight dent in it.

"Your uncle told me about the invitation he extended," he said a little gruffly, and she wondered if he'd been up all night, going over the evidence.

"Yes, well, I thought perhaps there was more evidence to be found on Frey's laptop." She hesitated, then decided not to hold back. Chase might not be willing to share, but she wasn't going to be so stingy. "After I talked to Gabby Cleret and Aissa Spring, I checked Frey's social media pages."

"And?"

"Well, turns out Paulo Frey was doing his darndest to earn himself the prize for the world's nastiest social media troll. The guy actively trolled women, especially when they didn't conform to his ideal of what the perfectly proportioned woman should look like, and was engaged in online warfare with dozens of his targets."

"Yeah, I saw that," Chase said, taking a break from checking the laptop.

She drew up a chair. "So I figure that maybe whoever killed him might have been one of his victims. Someone who decided enough was enough."

He stared at her. "And you hoped to find a lead on his laptop?"

She nodded. "There's only so much you can glean from a public Facebook page. If I could use his laptop to log into his accounts, I'll bet I'd find a treasure trove of stuff, and maybe a lead to his killer."

"Just what I was thinking," he admitted. "Which is why I've been going over his laptop half the night."

She didn't know why, but the fact that they'd shared the same idea somehow gave her a little thrill of excitement. "And? What did you find?"

"So far, nothing good," he said with a shake of the head. "You called it when you said the guy was a troll. Which is surprising for a writer of his stature. You would think he'd be afraid it would affect his sales."

"Did he have another account? In a different name, perhaps? An alias?"

"If he did, I haven't found it," he said, scooting over to allow her access to the computer. This greatly surprised her. Was he inviting her to actively join the investigation? Perhaps her mom's cooking had changed his opinion about nosy reporters whose last name happens to be Poole?

"Did you check his emails?"

"I checked a bunch of them, but there are thousands and thousands. To go through all of them will be a Sisyphus job."

"Then we better get cracking," she said with a grimace.

"Be my guest," he said, rising. "Coffee?"

"Black," she said, cracking her knuckles. Frey's laptop looked a little dilapidated, but then any laptop would, after spending a year soaked in human waste. It was a miracle the thing was still functioning. While Chase spent the next hour holed up in Uncle Alec's office for their morning briefing, she went through Frey's emails, checked his browser history, and generally tried to get a sense of what the guy had been up to in the weeks leading up to his death. And it was when she checked his bookmarks that she hit the jackpot. Apparently he'd been a member of some kind of cyber-vigilante group called the Army of No, Frey clearly one of its ringleaders and moderators.

As soon as she logged into their private forum, she discovered he'd been extremely active coordinating what he called campaigns against cast-offs, conducting online warfare on anyone he disapproved of. She found the conversations that had launched the coordinated campaign against Gabby Cleret, but it quickly became clear to her that the Army of No mainly sought out people with a higher body weight and outed them online, posting their pictures and referring to them with quite unpleasant epithets.

"Check this out," she said when Chase finally joined her. "This Army of No harassed dozens of women they considered overweight, actively attempting to shame them."

He read a few of the exchanges and shook his head. "This is so much worse than trolling," he finally said. "This is almost criminal."

She pointed at the screen. "I'll bet one of these victims decided to get even with their tormentor."

"But how did they even know he was behind these attacks? This entire group was working in complete anonymity, and Frey's name is never even mentioned."

Chase was right. Frey's involvement with the group was a strict secret, all the members using aliases. Frey's was Carb-

Killer, as he seemed to have developed a particular distaste for young women of a bigger size, and liked to single them out.

"Someone must have found out," she said.

"We have to compile a list of all the victims," Chase said.

She gave him an amused look. "Are we actually working this investigation together now, Detective Kingsley?"

He shrugged. "I'm starting to see that if I'm ever going to fit in in this town, I better adapt to the way things are done around here. And from what your uncle has been telling me you're a great researcher, so…"

"So you're allowing me to take part in the investigation?"

He studied her for a moment. "I'm drawing the line at you going out there and interviewing suspects—actively pursuing leads. But this…" He gestured at the laptop. "This is analyst's work, and I don't see why you can't give us your two cents. It's not as if there's any danger involved."

Annoyed, she said, "So I'm being relegated to playing second fiddle, is that right? You actually want to keep me from going out there and doing my job?"

"Doing *my* job," he corrected her tersely. "Interviewing suspects is police business, Miss Poole. And so is following leads. What would you do if a suspect turned violent? Or, God forbid, you actually confronted the killer and he or she turned the tables on you? You don't have a gun and even if you did, you're not trained to protect yourself." He shook his head adamantly. "You're not qualified and I want you off the street. Your uncle Alec feels the same way."

"I very much doubt that," she insisted.

"Look, I'm cutting you a lot of slack here," he said, gesturing at the computer. "And to be honest, I still think this is a bad idea."

"Well, thanks for nothing," she said, and got up.

Just then, her uncle stuck his head through the door.

"Frey's publisher is here. You want to be present while I do the interview? You too, Odelia," he said with a pointed look at Chase, who emitted an exasperated groan.

"Thanks for the vote of confidence, Uncle Alec," she said as she breezed past Chase and followed her uncle out of the small evidence room. On the way over to his office, she saw that Rohanna was busy cleaning the vestibule, moving and shaking to the music, as usual, and singing along to some unheard tune. She smiled. At least someone was having fun around here.

The interview with the publisher didn't take long. The man had been in town to pick up Frey's belongings that had been released, like his clothes, his suitcases and the printed-out copy of his manuscript. Uncle Alec was going to hang on to the laptop for a little while longer. When questioned why Frey's family didn't collect the writer's stuff, he said Frey was estranged from his family, and he was all he had. The publisher hadn't been happy with Frey, either, for he'd been having trouble finishing his new book, apparently too busy with his Army of No and his trolling to spend time writing.

When the interview was over, Chase and Odelia returned to the evidence. The moment she stepped inside, she clutched Chase's arm. "The laptop!"

"What?" Then his eyes swiveled to the table. "Oh, no."

The laptop they'd left on the table was gone!

The cop cursed under his breath, and instantly rushed out, Odelia right behind him. But when he asked Dolores, the dispatcher said no one else had been in there, and that she definitely hadn't touched that laptop.

Odelia stared around, and her eye fell on Rohanna, who was now busy dusting off a cabinet in the corner of the vestibule. It held pictures of Chief Alec holding up a very large bass, and several of his fishing trophies. She approached the cleaner, and when she tapped her on the shoulder, Rohanna started, and took out her earbuds. "Hey, honey. Everything all right?"

"Have you seen anyone pass by here? Something went missing from the evidence room," she explained.

But the cleaning lady shook her head. "I haven't exactly been paying attention. But I don't think I've seen anyone. Why don't you ask Dolores?"

She nodded, and quickly darted a glance at Rohanna's rolling cart. No sign of a laptop, of course. She dropped the crazy notion. "Thanks," she said, and shook her head at Chase, who'd been watching from a distance.

Judging from his frown, or the way he'd folded his arms across his chest, he wasn't happy about this. "I should have locked that room," he said now, as they walked back to the evidence room. "Never leave evidence unattended. It's the first rule," he added, scowling at her, as if he personally blamed her.

"What?" she asked. "So this is my fault now? I didn't take that computer."

"I know you didn't. But someone did. Someone snuck in here, managed to get past Dolores unseen, and snuck back out."

Rohanna's eye traveled to the window, which was open and didn't have any bars in front of it. "Do you think they might have gotten in through there?"

Odelia and Chase moved over to the window, and the detective opened it all the way so they could lean out. The view wasn't anything to write home about: a small patch of wasteland that once had been intended to be turned into a parking lot, but now was just a tangle of weeds. Someone could easily have come through there, hopped in through the window and absconded with that laptop. But who?

"It could have been thieves," Odelia suggested. "Kids wanting a free laptop."

But Chase shook his head grimly. "I doubt it."

"Yeah, actually so do I. Whoever stole that laptop must have known it contained information that might lead us to the killer."

He fixed her with a serious look. "Whoever took that laptop just might be the actual killer, Miss Poole."

And even though she rarely saw eye to eye with the burly cop, she had to admit he was probably right this time. Which meant the killer must have been watching them, following the investigation. Which also meant that the killer... was one of them. Not an outsider, but someone from Hampton Cove.

CHAPTER 22

I woke up feeling refreshed, and stretched happily. I couldn't remember having slept this great in quite a while. I opened one eye, saw that Dooley was still occupying the other side of the couch, and closed my eye again. Maybe I could squeeze in a couple hours more, now that I was going so well. But then I suddenly remembered Clarice's startling revelation of the previous day. She'd actually revealed the identity of the murderer! And we hadn't even told Odelia! Instantly, I was wide awake, and gave Dooley a poke.

He mumbled, "Juss... lemme... sleep... zzz."

I prodded him again, hissing, "We have to tell Odelia who the killer is!"

He opened his eyes lazily. "Killer? What are you talking about?"

"The killer! The Paulo Frey thing!"

He smacked his lips, then yawned, and as I watched, I could practically see his brain booting up, and grasping the meaning of my words. Suddenly his eyes snapped open, and he sat up with a jerk. "The killer! We have to tell Odelia!"

"That's what I just said," I said with a touch of exasperation.

I hopped gracefully from the couch and stretched my back, then strode languidly over to the stairs and started making my way upstairs. When I didn't find Odelia in the bedroom, I realized time had gotten away from us, and she'd already left for work. It was a lot later than I thought!

"She's gone," I said when Dooley sauntered into the bedroom. We both trotted down the stairs again, and were about to leave through the pet door when two cats came barging in. They were the last cats I wanted to see: Harriet and... Brutus. I leveled a disapproving look at the latter. This time he'd gone too far. "Brutus, this is my house, and I want you out of here."

Brutus gave me one of his trademark infuriating grins. "Wow, wow, wow. Now hold it right there, Maxie. Keep it cool, buddy. I'll have you know that I've come in peace."

"We've decided to offer you a peace treaty, Max," Harriet explained.

"So now you're on his side, are you?" I asked bitterly. I gave her a glowering look. "You're dead to me, Harriet. And you too, Brutus."

"Let's not say things we don't really mean, Max," said Harriet, clearly the negotiator in this standoff.

"Oh, but I mean them, all right," I said.

"You're dead to me, too," Dooley told Harriet.

"Oh, Dooley," said Harriet with an eye roll.

"No, but it's true. It's called calloosing, collosing..." He turned to me. "What is it called, Max?"

"I think you're probably referring to collusion with the enemy," I said. "Which is not something we take lightly."

"We don't take it lightly at all," Dooley confirmed.

"In actual fact I don't think you're our friend anymore,

Harriet. You've crossed a line that shouldn't have been crossed."

"It's one of those lines," Dooley agreed. "One of those uncrossable lines and you've gone and crossed it, Harriet."

"You're both being very immature," said Harriet. "We're all grown-ups here, so let's act like grown-ups."

"Speak for yourself," said Dooley. "I'm not a grown-up."

"Look. Last night during dinner it was obvious that Odelia and Chase are developing feelings for each other."

"I think the word lovebird is appropriate," said Brutus.

Harriet gave her new mate an adoring look. "They were exactly like lovebirds, weren't they?"

"They sure were, honey pie. Just like us."

"Oh, sugar plum," she cooed.

I thought I was going to be sick. "What's all this about last night?"

"Well, since you weren't there, you didn't see it, did you?" asked Harriet primly. "But Odelia and Chase made the loveliest couple."

I exchanged a look of panic with Dooley. "Couple?" I croaked.

"Lovebirds?" squeaked Dooley, on the verge of a panic attack.

"Yeah, you should have seen them," grunted Brutus with a chuckle. "Your regular Romeo and Juliet. Anyways, where were you guys last night?"

"None of your business," I snapped.

"If you have to know, we were investigating," said Dooley haughtily.

"Investigating?" scoffed Brutus. "In your sleep? Some investigation!"

"For your information, we cracked this case wide open," said Dooley. "In fact we cracked it all the way—like a nut."

"Dooley," I said warningly.

"You cracked the case?" asked Brutus. "You mean you caught the killer?"

"We most certainly did, sir," Dooley confirmed proudly.

"Dooley!" I said. "Shut up!"

"Yeah, shut up, Dooley," said Brutus. "Cause I'm pretty sure there's nothing to tell."

"We know exactly who the killer is," said Dooley, ignoring the anxious looks I was giving him, "because we found a witness to the crime. A very important witness."

At this point, Harriet asked, "You talked to a witness? Who was it?"

"Don't tell her, Dooley," I told him. "This is for Odelia's ears only. Besides, I thought Harriet was dead to you?"

"She is dead to me," Dooley confirmed, "but as long as she keeps asking me questions I can't not answer, can I? That would be just plain rude."

"Entering the house of another cat when you're not invited is rude," I said with a pointed look at Brutus. "And so is colluding with the enemy," I added with an even pointier glance at Harriet.

"Oh, I'm invited, all right," said Brutus. "Ain't that right, honey bunch?"

"I invited him," said Harriet. "This is my house, too."

"You've got some nerve," I said, shaking my head.

"I don't see why we can't all live together in perfect harmony," said Harriet, sounding like a seventies hit song. "Why we can't all simply get along and be friends."

"Because Brutus is a bully and a brute, and bullies and brutes don't get along with non-bullying brutes like us," said Dooley.

"Kicking a friend out of your house is kind of a brutish move, buddy," said Brutus.

"You're not my friend," I said stubbornly.

"A friend of a friend is a friend," he riposted.

"Well, since Harriet is dead to me that makes you…" I hesitated. This was all getting very confusing. "Anyway, I don't want you here so that's that."

Brutus grinned, displaying two sets of very sharp teeth. He patted my cheek with his paw. "Maxie baby. Your human and my human are practically a couple, which makes us more than friends. The moment those two lovebirds move in together you and me are going to be brothers, bubba! We be shacking up together. We be like homies, bro!"

"Yes, Max," gushed Harriet. "You should have seen Odelia and Chase last night. So in love. So Brutus is right. Very soon now we're all going to be living together, so why not let bygones be bygones and welcome him into the family?"

"Over my dead body," I growled, shaking off Brutus's paw.

Brutus moved in, and whispered in my ear, "That can be arranged."

I glared at him. "Why don't I simply tell Odelia I don't want you here?"

"That's it!" cried Dooley. "And then maybe she'll make Chase give you away!"

"In your dreams, buddy," growled Brutus.

"Odelia listens to what we tell her," I said. "And if we tell her we don't want you here, she'll give Chase an ultimatum: either get all loved-up and cuddly on her couch and watch *Blue Bloods* together, or get rid of you." I gave Brutus a sweet smile. "I wonder which way Chase is going to lean."

"We'll see about that," he said, but I could see a hint of doubt in his eyes. He probably never met a cat before who could make himself understood by his human, and it wasn't a gift he shared with us. He'd have no way of pleading with Chase to keep him, and I was pretty sure that if Dooley and I put our collective paws down, it was bye-bye Brutus.

"You wouldn't do that," said Harriet, aghast.

"I most definitely would."

"He's bluffing," said Brutus, giving me a nasty glare. "He's just trying to come between us, sweetie pie, and it'll never work."

Harriet seemed doubtful, though. She knew what we were capable of when push came to shove. But then she made up her mind and lifted her chin. "If you tell Odelia you don't want Brutus here, I'll tell her that I do want him here. That will make her think twice."

"You wouldn't do that!" I cried.

"Watch me," she said, narrowing her beautiful green eyes.

Dooley seemed even more taken aback. "You wouldn't go against family!"

"Of course not," she said sweetly, "since Brutus is my family now." She stared at the big, black cat adoringly.

What followed was a lot of cooing and lovebirding, and frankly it was too much to take on an empty stomach.

I realized this was going to prove a tougher fight than we'd anticipated. Not only had Brutus invaded our space and seduced our friend, but with Harriet he had gained a powerful ally to convince Odelia to accept him into our home. Odelia loved Dooley and me, but she adored Harriet. Everybody did. Because of that snowy white fur people always thought she was the most beautiful creature they'd ever laid eyes on, and would stop at nothing to give her what she wanted. If Harriet wanted Brutus introduced into the home, Odelia would do it, against my and Dooley's protestations.

Unless... I gave Dooley a nudge. "Let's go, buddy. We have a human to find and a job to do."

"But we can't leave these two here!" he cried. "This is our home!"

"And now it's mine," said Brutus with a smirk, and proceeded to stalk over to the couch, hop on, and make himself comfortable in my spot! Then he patted the space beside him. "Hop on, baby cheeks. Let's have a party."

Harriet giggled, and without awaiting my approval, hopped onto the couch, stretched out luxuriously, and lovingly gazed into her new mate's eyes.

"Oh, darn it," I muttered. "I can't take any more of this." And so I hurried out the pet door, Dooley in my wake. And as we rounded the house and made our way to the street, I said, "We have to do something about this."

"But what can we do? You heard Harriet. She'll vouch for him."

"I've got the perfect idea, Dooley," I assured him. "We'll simply tell Odelia we know who the killer is, but if she wants us to reveal the identity, first she has to kick that brute out of our house."

"You mean blackmail?" asked Dooley, eyes widening.

"Let's call it a bargaining chip."

He brightened. "I think it's a great idea! Do you think she'll go for it?"

"I'm sure she will. She's desperate to find that killer, so she'll give us whatever we want in exchange for the information."

We hurried along, now on a mission to save our home from this wicked intruder.

"I can't believe Harriet," Dooley lamented. "Who would have thought she'd betray us like this?"

"That's kitties for you," I said. "They see a handsome tom and they forget all about you."

"I thought she was our friend," said Dooley dejectedly.

"Well, she's our friend no more," I said with determination. "This is war, Dooley, and since she's colluding with the enemy that makes her our enemy, too."

"The enemy of our enemy is our enemy, right?"

I thought about this for a moment. "Not exactly."

Five minutes later, we strolled into the offices of the *Gazette*, and were surprised to find that Odelia wasn't there, seated at her desk as usual.

"Where is she?" asked Dooley. Then he gave me a horrified look. "Oh, no, Max! She's probably on Chase Kingsley's couch, kissing! Just like Harriet and Brutus!"

"I don't think so," I said musingly. "Chase is staying at Uncle Alec's place, and Odelia and Chase kissing on her uncle's couch simply seems… inappropriate."

"They could have rented a room! Humans do that! They love renting rooms!"

"Not so soon." Last time we saw Odelia she hated Chase Kingsley's guts, and I didn't think one family dinner would have made such a big difference, no matter what Brutus or Harriet said. I knew Odelia, and even though she'd brought home some weird specimens in the past, she was never one to kiss on the first date. "Let's check her other haunts," I said now. "I'll bet she's over at the doctor's office."

But when we went there, there was no sign of Odelia either. We stopped by the library next, and finally headed over to the police station. Now that Brutus had taken over my home, the station house was safe terrain once more. Brutus might be a lot of things, but he wasn't capable of being in two places at the same time. When we hopped onto our usual perch on Uncle Alec's windowsill, my heart leaped with joy when I saw Odelia holed up in there with her uncle and… Chase Kingsley. But just as we arrived, she left.

So we did the only thing a smart cat would do: we simply barged into the Chief's office through the window, plopped down on the man's desk, and, before his surprised eyes, hopped down and tripped after Odelia.

"Of all the…" the Chief grunted, then bellowed, "Odelia! Your cats are here!"

Odelia turned back, and was all smiles when she caught sight of us.

"Oh, hey, sweethearts," she said as she bent down and gave us a cuddle. "Finally up and awake, huh?"

"Oh, Odelia, we have so much to tell you!" Dooley cried.

"Yeah, we know who the killer is!" I added.

She gave us both a keen look but quickly rose again, and I immediately saw why: we were being watched with interest by Detective Kingsley.

"Are these your cats?" the burly cop asked.

"Yeah, they're mine," she said with a smile.

"And they just come barging in here like that?" he asked, raising his eyebrows.

"Your cat came barging into our house!" Dooley yelled.

But of course all Chase could hear was Dooley's plaintive mewling.

"Um…" Odelia stared down at me. I could see she was eager to listen to our story, but she couldn't very well do it now, with Chase watching on. To him it would sound like she was meowing, and might give the wrong impression. So instead she merely said, "They're very attached to me. Sometimes they follow me around all day."

"So you're not just a nosy reporter but a crazy cat lady too, huh?" he asked.

Odelia scowled at him, and I was happy to see that the two of them weren't an item. And if my extensive knowledge of human nature was anything to go by, it would take them a little while to get to that point.

"If I'm a cat lady, what does that make you? Crazy cat dude?" she asked.

Chase opened his mouth to respond, but he momentarily seemed lost for words, so he simply closed it again, and Odelia took the opportunity to stalk out of the office. Uncle

Alec, who'd laughed at his niece's comment, now said, "Shoo. Follow the lady, cats," and sent Dooley and me on our way.

I was pretty sure he was one of the few people who knew about Odelia's ability to talk to us, and I was glad he hadn't betrayed that secret to Chase. At least one person in this family wasn't selling out to the newcomers in town.

Dooley and I tripped after Odelia and joined her in a small empty office. The moment the door closed, she turned to us, and said, "I think I know who did it." And when she told us the name, both Dooley and I were surprised to find that she'd discovered the murderer's identity all on her own. When we confirmed that she was right on the money, she smiled. "Now to prove it…"

After she had left, Dooley and I shook our heads in dismay.

"There goes our bargaining chip," Dooley lamented.

CHAPTER 23

fter the disappearance of the laptop, it didn't take Odelia long to figure out that her initial theory was correct: there was something on that laptop that revealed the identity of the killer. And then it dawned on her. The Army of No. She quickly took out her phone and started googling. It was just a hunch, but her hunches often proved correct, so...

The mention of this Army of No had stirred a memory of a horrific event that had taken place a couple of years ago. Her father had been marginally involved at the time, and she'd even written an article about the tragedy.

She now walked into Uncle Alec's office and placed her phone on his desk and tapped it. "Check this out, Chief."

Her uncle quickly read the page indicated, and stared up at her. "No."

She nodded. "Yes."

"What's going on?" asked Chase, mystified by this exchange.

Her uncle gave her a slight nod, as he settled back in his chair and gazed out the window for a moment. She took a deep breath before launching into her story. "A couple of years ago, a young teenage girl was struggling with her weight, and finally confessed to her mom that she was being bullied at school for being overweight. After a lot of soul-searching, they finally consulted my dad, who advised they talk to a friend of his, a renowned psychologist in Bridge-hampton. They did, and over the course of the next couple of months became convinced that having weight loss surgery was the right thing to do. The girl was still in high school, so they decided to wait until after graduation so that nobody would be any the wiser when she suddenly started losing weight. She didn't want to attract attention to herself, and make a difficult and sensitive situation even harder."

"I remember the case," said the chief gruffly. "Poor kid."

"What happened?" asked Chase.

"Everything was going as planned, when suddenly the girl's upcoming medical procedure was outed on her school's Facebook page, pictures of her exiting the clinic where she'd been going to prepare for the gastric bypass surgery posted and the whole story being displayed for the whole school to see. It was a serious blow to the girl's self-esteem, which was already very low, and also for her mom, but they thought they could overcome it. But then the taunting started, and the name calling and the nasty comments. Finally, the girl couldn't take it anymore and…"

"It's all right, hon," said her uncle. "I'll tell the story if you want."

She shook her head, and continued, "A little over two years ago, when her mom came home from work, she found her daughter's body, a note on her desk telling her she was sorry to have caused her so much trouble, and that the world was much better off without her."

"Christ, that's horrible," said Chase, distractedly raking his fingers through his hair.

"Paulo Frey was behind the bullying campaign of the poor girl, I'm sure of it. I googled the affair, and the initial post and the pictures on the school page were posted by the Army of No. I think the girl's mother discovered that Frey was behind it. That he was the one responsible for her daughter's torment and subsequent suicide, and that in a fit of rage she decided to take her revenge."

"Who was this girl?" asked Chase now.

The Chief and Odelia shared a knowing glance, and finally the Chief said, "Lily Coral. Rohanna Coral's girl."

Chase's eyebrows rose. "Rohanna as in... the cleaner?"

"I think you'll find that the laptop is in her cleaning bucket," said Odelia. "She must have heard it was here and wanted to make sure we wouldn't find out about Frey and the Army of No and make the connection with her daughter."

"We better have a little chat with her," said the Chief now, and swiftly rose from behind his desk. And as they made to leave the office, Max and Dooley suddenly came barging in through the window, hopped onto Uncle Alec's desk, and announced to Odelia they had discovered the identity of the killer.

Instead of threshing this thing out in front of Chase, she ushered them into an empty office, and when they told her that Clarice had seen Rohanna drag the body of Paulo Frey into the cesspit that day, she had her confirmation. Now there was no doubt Rohanna Coral was the killer.

She hurried out of the office and told her uncle, "It's Rohanna, all right. We have to get her before she destroys the evidence on that computer."

"How..." asked Chase, a confused frown on his face.

"Like you said, I'm a cat lady," she said. "Cats inspire me. Now are you coming or not?"

Without waiting for a response, she sprinted down the

corridor to the vestibule, but Rohanna was nowhere to be found.

"Have you seen Rohanna?" she asked Dolores.

"Yeah, she left about twenty minutes ago."

She quickly went in search of the cleaning trolley, and found it in the small room where they kept the cleaning supplies. The bucket was still filled with soapy water and she plunged her hands in. "Nothing," she grunted. Of course. She looked up when Chase joined her. "She took the laptop."

"Let's go," he said curtly.

"I'll wait here, just in case she comes back," her uncle said.

She and Chase flew out the front door, and ran for their cars. Only now did she remember she'd parked hers in front of the *Gazette*. She eyed Chase's big pickup a little uncertainly. "Are you sure you can handle this thing?"

"Like a pro," he assured her. "Hop in."

"Hand me the keys. I'll drive."

He hesitated.

"I know where she lives."

After a moment's deliberation, he tossed her the keys. "You better not wreck my ride."

"I promise," she said, and got behind the wheel. Then, just when she was about to back out of the parking spot, Max and Dooley came running up. She quickly opened the door and they scooted in.

"You really are a cat lady," said Chase with a shake of the head.

"I'll take that as a compliment," she said, and then put the car in reverse and backed away from the curb, almost colliding with another car that was passing. "Oops," she said, then punched the accelerator, and raced away, tires spinning for purchase and burning rubber.

Chase appeared a little startled. "Do you always drive like this?"

"Only when I'm trying to catch a killer," she said.

She raced Chase's pickup through town, running a red light, which caused the cop to give her a censorious look but no comment, then a second light, which caused him to say, "I knew I should never have given you those keys."

They arrived at Rohanna's place, and she jumped the curb, causing the underbody of the truck to loudly grind in protest. Chase winced but said nothing, and they both hurried out and up the concrete steps to the front door. Rohanna lived on the second floor of a small housing project, and Odelia led the way.

Chase rang the bell and followed this up with a good hammering of his fist on the flimsy door. "Hampton Cove Police, ma'am. Open the door."

When there was no response, he drew his weapon and motioned for Odelia to stand back. Then he placed his foot against the door and gave it a good shove. The wood around the lock splintered and the door caved and then they were racing inside, Chase the first one through.

It didn't take him long to declare the place completely empty.

When they met at what was left of the front door, Odelia was thinking hard. Where could she have gone? It was hardly feasible she would have simply continued on with her regular schedule for the day. Or was it? In that case, she'd be cleaning her dad's office right now. She glanced over at Chase.

"What?" he asked, holstering his gun. "Where is she?"

She shook her head. "My best guess is my dad's office."

Chase gave her a meaningful look, and then they both raced back to the car. A couple of minutes and only one traffic violation later, she halted the car in front of the doctor's office with screeching tires, causing Chase to wince yet again. You'd think the man would have gotten used to her driving style by now. Barging inside, they walked straight up to the counter, where they were met by a grinning Gran. She looked delighted by this surprise visit.

"Hey there, Detective Kingsley. The doctor is busy, but if you want you can go over to examination room number two, and he can squeeze you in."

"Is Rohanna here?" asked Odelia, who had no time for this.

"Never saw her," said Gran. "Not that I miss her. Who needs a singing cleaning lady that can't clean? Or sing?" Turning to Chase, she plastered a smile on her wrinkled face. "Go on and strip down to your tighty whities, sonny jim. And if the doc can't see you immediately I'm sure I can accommodate you."

"In your dreams," growled Chase, and waltzed out again.

"Was it something I said?" yelled Gran, leaning over the counter to stare at Chase's retreating behind.

"Not now, Gran," she called out, leaving the old lady looking disappointed.

They both got back to the car, and Odelia saw that this time Chase was behind the wheel. When she glared at him, he said, "Hey, you got to drive last time. Now it's my turn. Besides, I don't want anyone else to get killed."

"I'll have you know that I'm an excellent driver," she grumbled, getting into the passenger seat. She thought for a moment. Where would Rohanna take that laptop? She'd thought she'd hidden it in that cesspit, until a nosy writer had dug it out and uncovered a crime. Now she would have to put it where no one would ever find it. And then suddenly she got it. "The graveyard," she said.

He lifted an eyebrow. "The graveyard? Are you sure?"

"Trust me. Now just go!"

And go he did, at a surprising rate of speed. Following her instructions, it didn't take him long to arrive at the town graveyard, and they both jumped out of the car, which Chase had parallel parked to perfection in front of the iron gates. The man had skills. If he didn't make it as a detective in this town, he could always become a valet.

His strong arm held her back before she could rush into the graveyard.

"Let me go first," he said, and took out his gun again.

She nodded her agreement. Never argue with a man with a gun.

"What are we looking for, exactly?" he asked.

"This is where Lily Coral was buried. I have a hunch it's where Rohanna is going to bury that laptop."

Chase gave her a curt nod of the head. "Stay behind me. This woman has killed once, she might do it again when cornered."

"I doubt she has a gun, Detective."

He gave her a grim look. "Better safe than sorry. You might be a pesky reporter and a cat lady, but that doesn't mean I want to see you killed. And definitely not on my watch."

"I think that's probably the nicest thing you've ever said to me."

"You're welcome. Now let's go!"

They moved stealthily through the wrought-iron gates and entered the graveyard, which consisted of gravestones dotting a smooth stretch of gently sloping lawn. Some of them were crooked and weathered with age, others looked newer. She hadn't been there in a while, the last time when she'd accompanied her gran to put flowers on her granddad's grave. When she heard plaintive mewls behind her, she saw that Max and Dooley had followed them into the graveyard. They didn't look happy. This was not their favorite hangout, she suspected, and they'd rather be home right now. So would she.

Chase gave her a quick glance, and she gestured with her hand. She knew exactly where Rohanna's daughter was buried, as she'd attended her funeral. In fact most of Hampton Cove had. Lily had been a sweet kid and well-liked, and if not for those few bullies who'd made her life miserable, she would still be alive today. It was a tragedy, but that still didn't give Rohanna the right to kill the man she held responsible. They approached the plot where Lily was buried, and they had a clear view of her gravestone, but of Rohanna there was no trace.

"It's right there," she whispered, pointing at the grave.

She stared down at the stone, and then saw that the earth had been disturbed behind it, as if someone had been digging. She knelt down, and after a moment's hesitation dug her hands in. Suddenly her fingers touched a solid object, and when she came away, she was holding the laptop.

She held it out to Chase, who grunted, "Good job."

Wow. Another compliment? This was practically a love fest.

But then suddenly she saw Rohanna looming up behind the cop, a heavy rock in her hand. And as she held up the rock, heaving it over Chase's head, she screamed, "Chase! Watch out!" But it was too late, and Rohanna would have knocked out Chase if not suddenly Max and Dooley had launched themselves at the woman, scratching her across the face and hands with mighty hissing sounds, claws extended.

Rohanna yelled in pain and dropped the rock, reaching for her face.

Instantly, Chase whirled around, and easily worked his attacker to the ground, then slapped a pair of handcuffs on the woman.

"Thanks," Odelia mouthed to Max and Dooley, who appeared extremely proud of themselves and their work in apprehending the Paulo Frey killer.

"How?" Rohanna asked when Chase hoisted her up. "How did you know it was me?"

Odelia held up the laptop. "Frey was the one who harassed your daughter, wasn't he? He was the one who ran the Army of No."

Rohanna nodded forlornly. "He was. He killed Lily. He might as well have handed her that rope and personally tied the noose around her neck. Him and that so-called army of his." She shook her head, tears now trickling down her face. "I had no idea Frey was behind it until I accidentally touched his laptop when I was cleaning his desk and the screensaver dissolved and revealed the website of the Army of No. I knew they were behind the harassment campaign against Lily."

"How did you know he was running it?" asked Chase.

"Usually when I cleaned the cabin, Frey took a walk in the woods. So when I saw the website I couldn't resist digging a little deeper. And that's when I saw the messages he'd posted as CarbKiller. He was the site's moderator! He'd used the same alias to post those hateful messages on Lily's school's page, so I recognized it immediately. I got so angry when I realized he was the one who'd killed my little girl! He was the one who'd caused all this."

She hung her head, and Odelia said, "I'm so sorry, Rohanna. But why didn't you simply talk to my uncle? He would have arrested Frey."

"You know as well as I do that guys like Frey are never punished," said Rohanna bitterly. "He's one of the happy few that can get away with murder. He would have hired the best lawyers money could buy and would have gotten off scot-free." She shook her head. "When he walked in, that smug smile on his face, I knew I was in the presence of pure evil. So when he took a seat at his desk, I grabbed the first thing I could find and hit him as hard as I could. For my daughter. So Lily's death wouldn't go unpunished."

Odelia stared at the woman, tears in her own eyes now. Two lives were destroyed, for Rohanna would probably go to jail for a long stretch. Unless a jury would consider these extenuating circumstances. She glanced down at the gravestone of the kind-hearted young woman who just wanted to live a happy life, if not for people like Paulo Frey, whose hate had destroyed her.

"You did it, Odelia," said Max.

"Yeah, you did it," Dooley chimed in.

"No, you did it," she whispered, making sure that Chase didn't overhear her. Even though the burly copper might be warming to her—and she to him, she had to admit—she didn't want her secret to get out. Uncle Alec might understand, but she was pretty sure Chase never would.

"Good job, Miss Poole," Chase grunted after he'd Mirandized Rohanna.

"Thanks," she said simply. "You too, Detective Kingsley."

He gave her one of his rare grins. "I think we're past that, don't you?" He held out his hand. "Chase."

"Odelia," she said, and shook his hand, also smiling now.

"Oh, dear," Max groaned behind her. "Looks like Brutus is here to stay."

EPILOGUE

One week after the events that had rocked Hampton Cove, Dooley and I were lazing around in the backyard, under the shade of an old tree near the back, when I suddenly saw Brutus and Harriet crossing over to us.

"Don't look now, Dooley," I muttered, "but here come the brute and his bride."

"What? Where?!" Dooley cried, and instantly started scanning the lawn.

We both stared at the couple as they drew nearer, and Dooley seemed on the verge of launching into a long tirade to make sure that the garden, at least, remained Brutus-free. But how could we keep anything Brutus-free these days? The cat was ubiquitous, as was the cop who owned him.

After Chase and Odelia had solved the Paulo Frey murder, the police detective had received a lot of accolades from the Hampton Cove brass. Not that we have a lot of brass around here. Just the Mayor and the members of the town council. It appeared that some residents had indeed launched a petition to remove Chase from active duty, and the council was still considering it. But after his remarkable

work catching the Frey killer, he'd earned himself a tempo-
rary reprieve, and had gained the admiration of a lot of
Hampton Covians, chief amongst them people like Aissa
Spring and Gabby Cleret who, it was rumored, had just
signed up for *Indiana Jones 2*.

Whether Odelia was for or against Chase wasn't clear to
me. She hadn't told us to stop trying to clear the man's name,
so that seemed to indicate she believed in his innocence and
wanted him to stay. On the other hand, she'd listened carefully when we told her Brutus wasn't our most favorite cat in
the world, and that we wanted him gone.

In other words, these were confusing times, and so for
now we did nothing, at least until Odelia made up her mind
and decided one way or the other. I, for one, wasn't going to
make an effort to keep the cop in town, especially as he came
with so much baggage. And this baggage was now bearing
down on us, his new girlfriend—our former friend Harriet—
in tow.

"Hey there, guys," Harriet said by way of greeting.

But since Harriet was still dead to us, and so was Brutus,
Dooley and I simply pretended not to hear her. We'd discov-
ered that Brutus hated the silent treatment, and so did
Harriet. Bullies can't stand being ignored.

Talking about bullies, Odelia had written the definitive
article on Paulo Frey, which had been picked up by the
national media. Apparently the man had been considerably
overweight himself as a kid, and had been mercilessly bullied
for it. As a teen he'd worked hard to lose that weight and had
eventually become a real gym rat, proud of his perfectly
honed physique. But he'd also developed an almost patholog-
ical hatred of people who didn't correspond with his idea of
physical perfection, and had launched his so-called Army of
No, an army of online trolls.

The big papers had all done stories on Frey, and the

upcoming trial that was going to decide Rohanna Coral's fate. I had high hopes that the judge and jury would be lenient. Her actions couldn't be condoned, but they could be understood. On this point Hampton Cove wasn't divided at all: pretty much the entire town had decided to rally behind Rohanna, and even chipped in to pay for a decent lawyer.

"She said, hey, you guys," Brutus said, repeating Harriet's words of greeting.

Dooley and I continued ignoring the two of them, hoping they'd simply go away. But of course they didn't. Some cats only need half a word to get your drift, but Brutus and Harriet obviously weren't amongst those.

"You guys, don't be like that," Harriet said. "Why can't we simply be friends?" she added, harping on her new favorite theme. "Brutus is actually a very nice cat once you get to know him." She emitted an involuntary giggle. "And I've gotten to know him very well this past week."

Dooley appeared on the verge of saying something, but I gave him a gentle prod in the ribs, and he clamped his mouth shut.

"Look," Brutus said, "I know that maybe I was a little heavy-handed when I first arrived, my human being a cop and all. What can I say? It's a hard habit to break. But I see now that Hampton Cove has so much more to offer than your usual rabble that requires policing. You've got some great cats out here, and I admit my methods, which may be appropriate for a crime-ridden big city, are not appropriate down here, where life is lived at a more leisurely pace."

Harriet rubbed his back encouragingly, and he gave her a grateful nod.

"What I mean to say is this: I'm sorry if I came across a little too strong, and I promise that from now on I'll try to see things your way." He gestured at Harriet. "My girlfriend has shown me that policing a town is about more than simply swinging a big stick. It's about befriending the locals. Earning their trust." He held out a paw. "And so I'm here to tell you that I'm ready to be your friend."

"If they'll have you," whispered Harriet.

He ground his teeth for a moment, then managed, "If you'll have me."

It was obvious they'd been rehearsing this shtick and that Harriet had been coaching him to say the right things, and as I stared at the outstretched paw of my nemesis, I wondered how best to respond to this new nonsense. Walk away? Or deliver a blistering rebuttal? And as I was pondering this, Dooley glanced at Harriet, flashed a big grin in her direction, and covered Brutus's paw with his own!

"I'm so glad you said that, Brutus!" he said "I just hate having to ignore my best friend Harriet!"

"Aw, Dooley," said Harriet. "You're my best friend, too."

The next moment, Dooley was rubbing his nose against Harriet's nose as if he hadn't seen her in ages, Brutus and I looking on in horror. Brutus because he didn't like other cats rubbing their noses against his girl's nose, and me because I couldn't believe Dooley had fallen for this nonsense.

"What about it, Max?" Brutus asked gruffly. "Forgive and forget?"

"I'm sorry, Brutus, but I simply cannot forgive a cat who thinks he can bully me in my own home."

"Fair enough. I'm a changed cat now, though."

"A changed cat? In one week?"

He glanced at Harriet. "Love has a way of changing you, you know."

"Oh, please. You can fool Dooley, but you can't fool me."

"Hey, I'm not kidding. This is true love right here, buddy."

I very much doubted whether a cat like Brutus was even capable of love. Don't you have to have a heart to be able to love?

At that moment, the doorbell rang, and moments later Chase walked out into the backyard, accompanied by Odelia, and as they took a seat on the patio, I could see how things were going to be. This Chase guy wasn't going to go away anytime soon. He was going to keep on coming, and judging from Odelia's expression as they chatted, at some point in the future they just might become more than mere friends. I'd seen that look before, when she brought Sam the crooked banker home, and again when she had that crooked cop over. Odelia might be a great human, but she had lousy taste in men. Which meant I was going to be saddled with Brutus for the foreseeable future.

Three cats were looking at me anxiously. Dooley, looking goofy now that he was friends again with Harriet. Harriet, who seemed both tense and hopeful, for I was her friend too, until she got involved with Brutus. And the bully, who seemed repentant, a look that didn't become him.

Finally I relented. "Oh, all right," I said, slapping Brutus's paw. "Forgive and forget." But before the celebration started, I added, "But I'm not going to be bullied in my own home. This is still *my* home and Odelia is *my* human."

"Fair enough," said Brutus with a grin. Then he leaned in and whispered, "But I'm still the cop around here, buddy, remember that. So what I say goes." He then gave me a fake smile, and I could see that all this nonsense about him being a changed cat had just been posturing for Harriet's sake.

"Oh, you sly…"

"Max!" cried Harriet.

"It's all right, gummy bear. Max and I are buds now. Aren't we, Maxie baby?"

My eyes darted from Dooley, giving Harriet's nose another rub, to Odelia, offering Chase a drink, to Brutus, eyeing me with a warning grin on his mug. Two could play this game, I thought, and plastered a smile on my face. "Of course we are. From now on we're one big, happy family."

"Oh, yay!" cried Harriet.

"Yay," snarled Brutus.

"And so three become four," Dooley said, beaming all over his face.

"The four musketeers!" Harriet yipped.

"Max can be our Porthos," said Brutus, and gave me a playful punch on the shoulder that hurt a lot more than it looked. "Right, Maxie baby?"

"Wasn't he the fat one?" asked Dooley.

"Ha ha," said Brutus.

"Ha ha ha," said Harriet.

"Ha ha ha ha," said Dooley.

Oh, goodness, I thought. So this was what hell looked like.

There was more playful ribbing and joking, and I wondered if I was the only one who could see Brutus for what he was: a nasty brute. And I wondered if his human was anything like him. If he was, Odelia was in for an unpleasant surprise. I gave the paw I'd touched Brutus with a good lick to wash away the foul stench.

This wasn't over yet. Not by a long shot!

THE END

Thanks for reading! If you want to know when a new Nic Saint book comes out, sign up for Nic's mailing list: nicsaint.com/news

EXCERPT FROM PURRFECTLY DEADLY (MAX 2)

Chapter One

Morning had arrived bright and early, and as usual I was having a hard time rousing my human. Odelia was still snoozing, even more reluctant than usual to throw off the blanket of sleep. She'd been stirring for the past hour, ever since her alarm clock had gone off and she'd unceremoniously silenced it with one well-aimed punch. In spite of all my nudging, meowing, and even scratching the closet door, she still showed no signs of getting out of bed.

She'd sat up half the night preparing for her interview today, but if she didn't get up now she'd miss it entirely. And it wasn't just any old interview either. For the first time in years, famous eighties pop singer John Paul George, aka JPG, had granted the Hampton Cove Gazette an exclusive.

John, whose star had shone so brightly back in the day, now lived as a recluse in his Hamptons mansion, only rarely venturing out. He was one of those pop deities and eighties icons whose name would go down in history along with Madonna, Michael Jackson, Prince and George Michael.

Originally he hailed from England, where they produce pop stars in a factory just outside London, but had settled in the Hamptons in the nineties, where he could enjoy sun and surf and an endless parade of boy toys.

"Odelia," I tried again, nudging her armpit with my head. "Oh, Odelia. Rise and shine, my pretty. John Paul George and legend are awaiting."

But instead of opening her eyes, she merely mumbled something and turned the other cheek, her blond hair fanning across the pillow and her green eyes remaining firmly closed. I stared down at her sleeping form. I could always give her a gentle nibble, of course. Maybe that would do the trick. Somehow I doubted it, though. When Odelia is asleep, only a shot from a cannon can wake her, or perhaps a piper beneath her window, like the Queen of England. I should know. I've been Odelia's constant companion for going on eight years now. My name is Max, by the way, and I'm a cat.

Finally, I'd had enough. I wasn't going to miss this interview, as JPG was as much a hero of mine as he was of Odelia's. The man had taken in more stray cats than the Hampton Cove animal shelter, and all of them had been given such a good life they'd spread the word far and wide: JPG loved cats and they, in return, adored him. Heck, if I wasn't so fond of Odelia I might have presented myself on the JPG doorstep, looking slightly bedraggled.

I'd talked to more than a few of the cats he'd taken in, and they said he actually served them pâté on a daily basis. The food supposedly melted on the tongue, and was so delicious and plentiful it sounded like feline paradise.

The thought of pâté decided me. I wasn't going to miss the opportunity to sample the best gourmet food in all of Hampton Cove just because Odelia liked to sleep in. So I jumped on top of her, prepared to give her a good back rub, claws extended. If that didn't do the trick, nothing would.

Just then, Dooley wandered into the room.

Dooley is Odelia's mom's cat, a beigeish ragamuffin and not the smartest cat around. He's also my best friend.

"Hey, Max," he said now as he leisurely strode in. "What's up?"

"What's not up is the more apt question," I grumbled, gesturing at Odelia, who turned and clasped her pillow with a beatific expression on her face.

"Aw, she looks so sweet," said Dooley, looking on from the bedside carpet.

"We've got an important interview scheduled in an hour, and if she doesn't get a move on she's going to miss it."

"One hour? She can make that. Easy."

"Well, unless she gets up right now she won't," I insisted.

And then I got it. Maybe we could serenade her. Dooley and I had recently joined the cat choir. We got together once a week to rehearse, and even had our own conductor. We sang all the old classics, like *Cat's in the Cradle*, *Year of the Cat*, *What's New Pussycat* and things like that. The good stuff. Since we usually practiced at night, though, we were having a hard time finding a regular spot to get together, as the neighbors didn't seem to appreciate our nascent talent as much as we did.

"What was that song we did last night?" I asked Dooley.

He looked up at me. "Mh? What song?"

"For the cat choir. What was that last song we did? The one that made the mayor throw that old shoe at you?"

Dooley frowned at this, and rubbed the spot on his back where the shoe had connected. "That wasn't funny, Max. That really hurt, you know."

"Yeah, but what was the song?" I insisted.

"*Wake me up before you go go*," he said. "The old Wham! classic."

"Of course," I said with a grin. "Let's do it now. I'm sure it'll be a nice way to wake Odelia up, and put her in the right mood for her interview."

I jumped down from the bed, and took up position next to Dooley. We both cleared our throats, just like our conductor Shanille, Father Reilly's tabby had taught us, and burst into song.

"*Wake me up before you go go*," I howled.

"*Don't keep me hanging on like a yo-yo*," wailed Dooley.

And even though we hadn't practiced the song a lot—the mayor's shoe had kinda ruined the moment—I thought we were doing a pretty good job. It probably wouldn't have carried George Michael's approval, as cats don't exactly sing like humans. When we sing, it sounds more like... a bunch of cats being strangled. Nevertheless, the effect was almost magical. We hadn't even gotten to the chorus yet, when Odelia buried her head in her pillow, then dragged the pillow over her head, and finally threw the pillow at us.

"Stop it already, you guys. You sound horrible!" she muttered.

"It's Wham!," I told her. "So it can't be horrible. And if you don't get up right this minute, you're going to be late for your important interview."

At this, she darted a quick look at her alarm clock, and uttered a startled yelp. The next moment she scrambled from the bed, practically tripped over Dooley and me, and raced for the bathroom.

"Shit shit shit shit shit!" she cried. "Why didn't you wake me?!"

"Well, I tried!" I called after her. "And failed."

"You think she doesn't like our singing?" asked Dooley,

who's very sensitive about his singing skills. Coming after the shoe incident, Odelia's critique had clearly rattled him.

"I'm sure she loved it," I told him, padding over to the window.

Unlike humans, us cats don't need to spend time in the bathroom, or apply makeup, or put on clothes. We do spend half of our lives licking our butts, but apart from that, being a cat is a lot easier than being a human.

"I sensed criticism," Dooley said now, staring at the door through which Odelia had disappeared. "She said it sounded horrible, Max. Horrible!"

"She's not awake yet," I said. "She doesn't know what she's saying."

I hopped up onto the windowsill and watched the sun rising in the East. Outside, in the cherry tree that divided Odelia's garden from her parents', cute little birdies were chirping, singing their own songs, and fluttering gaily. I licked my lips. Coming upon the thoughts of pâté, the sight was enough to make my stomach rumble.

Dooley joined me, and we both stared at the birdies, twittering up a storm. There's nothing greater than waking up in the morning and seeing a flock of little birdies fluttering around a tree. It lifts my mood to such heights I can't wait to get out there and meet the world head-on. And the birdies. I saw Dooley felt the same way, for his jaw had dropped and he was drooling.

"So how's things over at your place?" I asked.

His happy gaze clouded over. "Rotten. That Brutus is spending more and more time at Marge's place than he does at his own."

Brutus was the black cat that belonged to Chase Kingsley, who was a new cop who'd recently moved to Hampton Cove. He was staying at Chief Alec's, Odelia's uncle, until he got a place of his own, but Brutus seemed to feel more at ease at the Pooles than at Uncle Alec's. And then there was the fact that he was dating Harriet, of course, Odelia's Gran's white Persian, who lived in the same house. One big, happy family. Except that it wasn't.

It had been a tough couple of weeks, Brutus being some kind of dictator, who liked to think he had to lay down the law to us plebeians. And since Dooley had always been sweet on Harriet himself, he was pretty much in hell right now.

"Brutus still being such a pain in the butt?" I asked.

Dooley nodded forlornly. "Last night he told me that from now on I should sleep on the floor. That all elevated surfaces were strictly reserved for him. Something about him having to have the best vantage point in case the house was being burglarized. I swear that cat is driving me up the wall."

"That's just plain silly," I said, shaking my head. Both Dooley and I had been wracking our brains trying to come up with a way to take Brutus down a peg or two. But as long as Harriet was his girlfriend, that was kinda hard, especially since Harriet is pretty much the most beautiful cat in Hampton Cove, and whatever she says goes with humans.

"You can always sleep on my couch, Dooley," I said magnanimously.

In spite of Brutus's efforts to take over my house as well, so far he hadn't succeeded. Fortunately Odelia still listened to me, and kicked him out when he became too much for me to handle. Oh, that's right. Didn't I tell you? Odelia is one of those rare humans who understands and speaks feline, on account of the fact that one of her forebears was a witch or something. Her mother and grandmother share the same gift, which comes in handy from time to time. Like when I have some scoop to share. You see, Odelia works for the Hampton Cove Gazette, and with the exclusive scoops we provide her she can practically fill the entire paper, earning her a reputation as the best reporter in town. She's also the only reporter in town, apart from Dan Goory, the Gazette's geriatric editor and Odelia's boss.

Finally, Odelia came shooting out of the bathroom, smelling deliciously of fresh soap, and looking fresh as a daisy. For the occasion she was wearing a T-shirt that read 'John Paul George for President,' beige slacks and her usual Chuck Taylors. She was also wearing a look of panic over how late it was.

"If you're coming, you better get a move on!" she yelled as she hurried down the stairs, then came pounding up again to snatch her smartphone from the nightstand and raced out again.

"Looks like she's going to have to skip breakfast," I told Dooley.

"And coffee," he said. "I wonder how she's going to survive without her daily dose of caffeine."

"I'm sure she'll manage," I said, reluctantly dragging my eyes away from the feathery feast outside my window, where the birds were still tweeting up a storm. Odelia had once made us swear never to kill a bird, and even though it killed us, we'd kept up our bargain so far. It was hard, though. Very hard. But in exchange for curbing our innate savagery she got us some of those delicious cat treats from time to time. What can I say? Life's a trade-off.

Dooley and I gracefully dropped down to the floor, and languidly made our way to the landing, then descended the stairs. While Odelia rummaged around, grabbing her notes she'd prepared for the interview, her recorder and a couple John Paul George CDs she wanted signed, and dumped it all into her purse, I gobbled up a few tasty morsels of kibble, took a few licks of water, and then waited patiently by the door until Odelia was ready.

I knew it would take her at least three runs to fetch all of her stuff. She was one of those humans who are extremely disorganized. So when she finally yelled, "Ready or not, I'm going!" Dooley and I had been waiting ten minutes. We were eager, actually. Hot to trot, in fact. It's not every day you meet your idol, and I knew Odelia was as excited as I was to meet JPG in the flesh. She because she'd grown up with his music, and I because I was finally going to find out if the rumors about that pâté were true. No matter who I had to bribe, I was going to sample me some of those delicious goodies.

Dooley and I hopped into Odelia's old pickup, and made ourselves comfortable on the backseat while she put the car in gear with a dreadful crunching sound that indicated she'd just destroyed what was left of the transmission. Miraculously, the car still lurched away from the curb, and five minutes later, we were cruising down the main drag of our small town.

Hampton Cove was just waking up, and Main Street was still pretty much deserted as we came hurtling through at breakneck speed. As a driver, Odelia is something of a legend in town. She's probably had more fender benders than all the other residents combined, and the only reason she hasn't been forced to declare bankruptcy to avoid paying traffic tickets is because her uncle is chief of police and tends to turn a blind eye to his niece's peccadillos. He has repeatedly told her to be more careful, but she insists the problem doesn't lie with her. She happens to be a great driver. It's other road users insisting on getting in her way that create all that trouble for her.

Meanwhile, we'd zoomed through Hampton Cove and were now racing along a stretch of road that took us along the coastline and the fancy mansions that the rich and famous had built for themselves. Dooley and I glanced out at them with relish. We had friends who lived here, and sometimes described the kind of lifestyle they'd grown accustomed to. It was enough to boggle the mind. Not that we're jealous cats, mind you. Odelia Poole is probably among the nicest and most decent and loving humans a cat can ever hope to adopt, but a monthly spa retreat just for cats? Cat birthday parties where all the other cat owners bring special treats? A walk-in closet just to fit all the costumes and fancy outfits? Like I said, it boggled the mind.

We finally arrived at the villa that was the home of John Paul George, eighties icon, and we were surprised to find that the entrance gate was wide open, a car haphazardly parked right next to it. As we rode past, we saw that inside the car a male figure was sleeping, his head slumped on the steering wheel, and recognized him as Jasper Pruce, JPG's long-suffering boy toy.

"Someone was naughty last night," Odelia said, lowering her sunglasses to get a good look at the guy. "JPG made him sleep outside, apparently."

"Don't humans usually have to sleep on the couch when they're bad?" asked Dooley, who looked confused. Human behavior often confuses him.

"Looks like the couch was occupied," I said, shaking my head.

We rode up to the house, and Odelia parked in the circular drive, right next to a fountain with a statue of JPG as a nude angel, spewing water out of its tush. We all hopped out and sauntered up to the front door. Odelia rang the bell, and we could hear it resonate inside the house. But even after she'd repeated the procedure, nobody showed up to answer, and she frowned.

She tried to peek through the glass brick wall next to the door, but it was impossible to get a good look because of its opaqueness.

She rang the bell again, biting her lower lip. "I hope he

didn't forget about our appointment. It has taken me months to nail down this exclusive."

"Want us to have a look round the back?" I asked.

"Would you? I don't dare to go there myself. What if he's sunbathing in the nude and accuses me of trespassing? I'll never hear the end of it."

Dooley and I moved off on a trot and rounded the house. We arrived at the back, where a large verandah offered a glimpse of the inside, but saw no evidence of anyone sunbathing, in the nude or otherwise.

"Oh, look," said Dooley. "He's got a pool."

And indeed he did. We walked over to the pool to take a closer look, and that's when we saw it: a lifeless figure was floating facedown in the center of the pool, completely in the nude, and judging from the large tattoo of two mating unicorns on his left buttock and a rainbow on the right, this was none other than John Paul George himself. I remembered seeing that tattoo when Odelia was researching the singer last night, and even though it looked slightly saggy now, having been tatted during the pop sensation's glory days, it was still recognizable.

John Paul George, eighties boy wonder, was either breathing underwater, or he was dead.

Chapter Two

After we told Odelia what was going on, we pussyfooted back to the pool area, this time with Odelia right behind us. But even as we led the way, she told us, "This is a very bad idea, you guys. I shouldn't be back here."

It seemed like a weird thing to say for a top reporter, and I told her so.

"I don't know," she said. "Strictly speaking this is trespassing. And what's even worse, if what you're saying is true and

John Paul George is dead and floating in his pool, I might get into a lot of trouble here."

It was the arrival in town of that new cop, I knew. The old Odelia wouldn't have thought twice about trespassing, and the fact that a famous celebrity was dead in their pool would only have made her run faster. But Kingsley's arrival had apparently robbed her of her journalistic instincts.

"Look, the guy invited you," I said. "So you're not trespassing."

"Well, that's true, I suppose."

"Besides, officially you don't know that he's dead. You didn't hear it from us. You just wondered why he didn't answer the door, you got worried, and you thought you'd better check, in case something had happened to him."

"I like your thinking," she said, nodding. We'd walked around to the back of the house, and she gasped when she caught sight of the floating body. The last doubts as to whether the guy was snorkeling were removed: for one thing he wasn't equipped with a snorkel, and for another, no one can hold their breath for that long, and certainly not a fifty-year-old drug-addled pop star.

"Oh, God," said Odelia as she approached the pool. Then she proved that she was still the ace reporter I knew her to be: instead of a pool hook, she grabbed her smartphone and snapped a few shots of the deceased.

"Do you think he's dead?" asked Dooley.

"I think that's a pretty safe assumption," I said.

"Is it John Paul George?" was his next question.

I pointed at the tattoos on his behind. "See those tats?"

Dooley nodded. "Uh-huh."

"Only a pop star who's consumed massive amounts of dope and booze would ever even think of having those particular tattoos inked on his butt."

"Dope?" asked Dooley. "What is dope?"

"It's, um, like pâté for humans, only not as good for you."

"We have to call the police," said Odelia.

We all stared down at the floating body. The former teenage heartthrob was now twice the size he'd been in his eighties heyday. No wonder he was rarely seen these days, and never granted any interviews. One stipulation he'd given Odelia for her exclusive was no pictures, and I could see why. He probably wanted to preserve the image of his youthful self to his fanbase, not allowing them to see the extended version of himself he'd turned into.

Odelia pressed her phone to her ear, and when the call connected, said, "Dolores? Can you tell my uncle there's been an accident at John Paul George's place? And tell him to send an ambulance. Yeah, he's dead."

While she gave the dispatcher some instructions, my eye wandered to the pile of glass vials on a table, the dozen or so empty champagne bottles on the pool chairs and the ashtrays full of reefers. That must have been some party.

"Oh, and can you also tell him JPG's boyfriend is dozing in a car in front of the estate. Maybe he's got something to do with this tragedy. Thanks, hon."

She disconnected and crouched down at the edge of the pool. It was obvious that the demise of one of pop music's greats had strongly affected her, to the extent she'd stopped snapping pictures, probably out of respect.

Just at that moment, a cat came walking out of the house. She was a beautiful Siamese, and said, "What's all this noise? And who are you people?" Then she caught sight of the man floating in the pool and faltered. "Is that…"

"Afraid it is," I told her, and watched her approach the pool wearily.

"Is he… dead?"

"Afraid so," I repeated, studying her closely.

She jerked back when the truth hit her. "Oh, no. Johnny's dead?"

"Looks like it," I said. "How long had you known him?"

The segue wasn't very smooth, I admit, but that's what you get from living with a reporter: you start acting like one yourself.

She shook her head distractedly. "Long enough to know that this isn't right." She plunked down on her haunches, and stared at her dead human.

"Is it true that he fed you guys pâté every day?" asked Dooley.

She looked up sharply. "What kind of a question is that? Who are you?"

"The name is Dooley," he said, scooting forward, probably to rub his butt against hers. But the look she gave him quickly dissuaded him.

"You're trespassing, Dooley," she said simply. "Please leave."

I shot Dooley a censorious glance and he lifted his shoulders. "What?"

"You can't ask the cat of a recently deceased human about pâté," I hissed.

"Why not? Isn't that what we came here for?"

"Well, you just can't," I whispered. Even though I was pretty curious about that pâté, too, of course. But there's a time for pâté and now wasn't it.

Just then, two more cats came sauntering out of the house, and then two more, and before we could say hi to the first bunch, we'd been joined by a dozen cats, and they all sat staring at the dead man. Then, as one cat, they all started mewling plaintively, letting their torment be heard across the pool.

Dooley gave me a curious look, but instead of explaining to him that this was what cats did when their owner suddenly passed away, and especially an owner as generous with the pâté as John Paul George apparently was, I decided to join in the ritual. After a moment's hesitation, so did Dooley, and before long, we were both howling along, our cat choir practice finally coming to good use. Even though JPG hadn't been our human, we could certainly understand the distress that comes with having to say goodbye to a beloved human, and as we mewled up a storm, Odelia simply sat there.

Soon, our howls mingled with the sounds of a police siren, and before long we were joined by Chief Alec, Chase Kingsley, and other members of the Hampton Cove Police Department. They all walked up to Odelia and for a moment simply stood staring at us cats, as we continued our cater-wauling. Then, just as abruptly as we'd started, we broke off, and one by one the cats all drifted back inside. They'd said their goodbyes and the show was over.

Dooley and I decided to follow the others inside and glean what information we could from them. That, and we desperately wanted to take a look at the house, of course, and how the other cats lived.

The house itself was a genuine mansion, with nice hard-wood floors and huge portraits of the singer adorning every room. The man had apparently possessed a healthy dose of self-love, for he was staring down at us from every wall in every room we passed through. I quickly trotted after the group of cats as they made their way to what looked like a family room. At least it was where a collection of cream-colored sofas were gathered around an outsized coffee table that held a collection of outsized coffee-table books, all sporting pictures of nude males on the covers and all visibly well-thumbed.

The cats hopped up onto the couches and the coffee table and made themselves comfortable. In one corner of the room stood a white grand piano, and here, too, several cats stretched out and chilled.

I decided to follow the Siamese, who seemed the only one willing to talk, and saw she'd sauntered into what looked like a recording studio off the family room. A lot of studio equipment indicated this was some kind of home studio, with an actual sound studio, recording booth and plenty of instruments placed against the far wall. I also saw enough gold and platinum albums to fill a hall of fame. This was JPG's personal hall of fame, that was obvious. The Siamese sat next to an acoustic guitar that was placed on the floor, next to a couple of bean bags, a stack of music paper nearby.

"Was this where he composed his music?" I asked.

She nodded, and appeared on the verge of tears.

"He was a great artist," I told her. "An icon of his generation."

She looked up sharply. "What do you mean, his generation? He was the musical icon of this century, and the last. The greatest living artist, bar none."

"Well, there are others," Dooley argued. "I mean, what about The Beatles? The Stones? Dylan?" He shut up when she gave him a dirty look.

"None of them were as influential and as talented as Johnny," she said, and it was clear we were dealing with an actual groupie here. A super fan.

"So what happened last night?" I asked, deciding it was perhaps better to grab the bull by the horns, or the Siamese by the ears, as was the case.

She shook her head. "He was partying hard, as usual. He'd just had another fight with Jasper, and he was overcompensating."

"Jasper?" mouthed Dooley.

"The boyfriend," I mouthed back. "We saw that. He's parked out front."

"That often happen?" asked Dooley.

She nodded. "They'd been fighting a lot lately. Jasper didn't like that Johnny consumed so much… candy. He said that wasn't what he'd signed up for. But Johnny said it gave him the boost he needed to create his music."

"Candy?" asked Dooley.

"Dope," I told him. "So Johnny still recorded?"

"Oh, yes, he did," said the Siamese with a smile. "Johnny must have recorded hundreds of songs since I came to live with him. All masterpieces."

"I'll bet," Dooley muttered, earning himself another scowl.

"When was this?" I asked.

She flickered her eyelashes at me. "Is that a roundabout way of asking me how old I am?"

"Um…"

"Johnny took in any stray that wandered into his home," she continued with a wistful smile. "But he got me from a proper breeder five years ago and I have the pedigree to show for it. Not that it matters." She sighed. "Johnny was the most generous human a cat could ever hope to come across. He loved all of his children, as he called us, and cared for us deeply." Once again, it looked as if she was on the verge of tears, and Dooley and I stared at her sheepishly.

I would have gone over and said, 'There, there,' but somehow I doubted whether this would go over well with this feisty and proud Siamese.

"Do you think there might have been foul play involved?" I asked instead.

She stared at me with her beautiful blue eyes. "I doubt it. Who would want to harm such a sweet and charming man? Everybody loved Johnny, and not just us cats. He had lots of friends, and partied every single night."

"What about his boyfriend?" I asked. "You said yourself he was jealous."

"Impossible. They might have had their differences, but Johnny and Jasper loved each other, in their own way. They had an understanding."

"Which was?" asked Dooley.

She eyed him angrily. For some reason she didn't seem to like Dooley. "I don't expect you to understand, but they gave each other freedom and respect. Jasper knew Johnny was an artist and needed his space, so he happily gave him what he needed. He knew Johnny would never hurt him intentionally, but that he had certain... needs, and so he turned a blind eye."

"Right," I muttered, remembering the pile of glass vials and the reefers and the bottles of champagne. I now wondered what had been in those vials.

"How many people were here for the party?" I asked.

She shrugged. "Maybe a dozen. Only one stayed the night, though."

"And it wasn't Jasper," said Dooley.

"Like I said," she snapped. "They had an understanding."

"Though last night they also had a fight," I reminded her.

"Yes, Jasper told Johnny he was fearing for his health. He was using too much and too frequently."

"Using what?" I asked.

"Some... substance. It came in clear glass vials. It made Johnny happy."

And now it had made him dead, I thought. "So who was the lucky young man who got to stay behind last night?"

"No idea. I was roaming the beach, and so were most of the others."

"So who—"

"George told me. George never goes anywhere."

"And who is this George?"

"He's Johnny's first cat. He brought him over from England years ago."

"George must be pretty old by now."

She laughed. "Don't tell him that to his face. George is very vain."

"Where can we find him?"

"You won't get anything useful out of him," she said as she started strumming the guitar with her nails. "George is extremely loyal."

"We'll see about that," I muttered. "Thanks, Miss…"

"Johnny always called me Princess," she said, and sighed. "I'll miss him."

I could very well imagine. If my human died one day, I'd miss her, too. Us cats might have the reputation we're selfish and we don't care about humans, but that's a filthy lie. We do care about our humans. We just don't care to show it as much as dogs do, with their exaggerated slobbering and posturing.

Dooley and I left the distraught Princess and made our way back to the family room, where the other cats were still looking glum. I wondered what was going to happen to them. I imagined JPG must have made provisions in his will for his beloved felines, and they would all be taken good care of.

"This makes me sad," said Dooley, gesturing at the sad-looking cats.

"Yeah, it's not a barrel of laughs," I agreed.

We both stared up at a life-sized portrait of the pop singer. It depicted him in his prime, with naked torso, looking like a young god. At his feet a large red cat sat perched, staring haughtily at the viewer.

I pointed at the cat. "I'll bet that's George."

"You want to have a chat with George? Or check out that pâté first?"

It was a tough choice. We'd come here for the pâté, obviously, but we also had an obligation to Odelia to find out as much as we could from the feline population about what had happened here last night. Finally, I said, "That pâté isn't going away, so we better talk to George first."

"Didn't you hear Princess? George has been here for years. He's the one who's not going away. That pâté might be gone by the time we find it." He shook his head. "A distressed cat eats, Max. It's called stress-eating."

He was right, of course. Still… "Look, this talk with George won't take long, and I'll bet there's plenty of pâté. JPG didn't stint on anything."

"Why don't we split up? I'll look for the pâté and you look for George."

"Yeah, right," I scoffed. "So you can eat all the pâté? I don't think so."

"I wouldn't do that, Max. I'm not a glutton. I'd simply sample the stuff. Just to see if it's as good as advertised. And if it is, I'll leave some for you."

"That's very generous. You know what? I'll look for that pâté. You find George."

"You're a much better interrogator, Max. Cats open up to you."

"Why don't we find that pâté together," I finally suggested, "before it's all gone."

"Now you're talking. Hey, look," he said, gesturing at a lone ginger cat that shuffled out of the family room. It was the fattest cat I'd ever seen.

"That must be George," I said.

"Let's ask him where the pâté is," Dooley said happily.

"Good call," I grunted, a low rumble in my tummy deciding me.

Hey, we're cats. We're willing to do whatever it takes to help out our humans. As long as you keep us properly fed and hydrated.

Chapter Three

Odelia got up to meet her uncle and Chase. She'd been seated on one of the pool chairs, thinking deep thoughts about the fleetingness of life.

She gestured at the man floating in the pool. "This is how I found him."

"And what were you doing here, exactly?" asked Chase, none too friendly as usual. Ever since the burly cop had moved to Hampton Cove, he and Odelia had locked horns over his idea that the citizenry had no place in police investigations, whereas she felt she was simply doing her duty to the Hampton Cove population by reporting on any crime that was committed here.

"I had an interview with him, and when he didn't answer the door…"

"You decided to break in," Chase supplied.

"I was worried when he didn't answer the door," she said with some heat. Why did this guy insist on rubbing her the wrong way? "So, yes, I decided to walk round the back and see what was going on. What's wrong with that?"

"I don't believe you have to ask," he grumbled, shaking his head.

Uncle Alec knelt next to the pool. "That's Johnny, all right," he said.

"How do you know?" asked Chase, joining him.

The Chief pointed. "See those tattoos? Johnny was famous for those. They were on one of his best-selling albums. Unicorns and Rainbows."

"I remember," said Chase, nodding, and started singing softly. "*Unicorns and rainbows. That's the way the wind blows. Loved you in those funky cornrows…*"

Now it was Odelia's turn to give him a curious look.

"What? I loved that song," said Chase.

"I had you pegged as a country and western kind of guy. Not a JPG fan."

"Hey, I was young once."

"Hard to imagine," she muttered. She saw that her uncle was checking the glass vials on the poolside table. "What do you think those are?"

"If I had to venture a guess I'd say GHB," he said.

"Liquid G? The date rape drug?"

He nodded. "It's supposed to supply a great high. Used by ravers."

She imagined her uncle saw these drugs all the time during the summer, when teenagers descended upon the Hamptons in droves to party all night.

Chase walked over and eyed the vials closely. He put on plastic evidence gloves and carefully picked one up and sniffed it. "You could be right, Chief."

Uncle Alec nodded. "It's no secret that JPG was a heavy user of the stuff. It's been rumored for years he got his stash of GHB right here in town, but I've never been able to pinpoint who exactly his dealer was."

"If it is Liquid G," said Chase, "it might be what killed him."

More people arrived now, and Odelia recognized one of them as the medical examiner, a scruffy-looking paunchy man with electric gray hair. Under his instructions they carefully dragged the body of the late singer to the side, then hoisted him up out of the water and placed him on a plastic tarp. The sight was disconcerting to say the least, and Odelia uttered an involuntary gasp. She hadn't seen any pictures of the singer in years, and since he was completely naked, she now got to see all of him and it wasn't flattering. The man was bloated, and it wasn't because he'd been in the water all night either, she guessed. JPG had obviously let himself go, and looked nothing like his trim and sexy self. Of course that had been thirty years ago.

The medical examiner quickly and expertly checked the body, while Chase and Uncle Alec went over the crime scene, along with the other officers. Odelia, meanwhile, stood back. She might be there in a non-official capacity because her uncle allowed it, but that didn't mean she could actively participate in the investigation.

"Did you check the boyfriend at the gate?" she asked when Uncle Alec wandered over.

"Yes, we did. Apparently they had some kind of a fight last night, and he drove off, only to return and spend the night in his car. From what I can tell, it wasn't the first time. There have been complaints from neighbors about screaming fights the last couple of months. They were not a happy couple."

"Poor guy. He had to sit back and watch his boyfriend invite over these…" She gestured at the bottles of champagne and the vials. "Friends."

"Male escorts is the word," said Uncle Alec. "You don't have to pay friends to have sex and party all night. You have to pay these guys, though."

"Kinda sad for a man like JPG to lead a life like this, don't you think?"

"Yes, well, if this was the life he chose, that was entirely his business," said the Chief, who believed in the age-old adage of live and let live, as long you didn't hurt others. It was a credo that helped him cope with the celebrities that lived in these beachfront properties, and sometimes liked to do stuff that no clean-living, well-meaning Hampton Covian would.

"What do you think happened?" she asked now.

He scratched his scalp. "I think Johnny had himself a

great party here last night, lots of booze and dope, he overdosed and drowned."

"So you think it was an accident?"

He raised his eyebrows, and wandered over to the coroner. "Abe?"

"Well, he didn't drown, that's for certain," said the coroner.

Both Odelia and her uncle looked at him in surprise.

"No water in the lungs as far as I can tell," the coroner explained. "Though I'll have to get him on my slab to know for sure."

"Overdose?" the chief asked.

The coroner looked up at them from his position next to the body. "If it was an overdose it wasn't from GHB, if that's what you're thinking. This man died of a seizure of some kind. But like I said, I'll know more later on."

Both Uncle Alec and Odelia's eyes flashed to the pile of vials on the table.

The coroner nodded. "I'll have them examined. See what they contain."

Chase, who'd been checking around the pool area, returned with two items dangling from his gloved fingers. One was a bright red Mankini, the other looked like a used condom. He gave the chief a grim-faced look. "Plenty more where this came from," he grunted. "At least five more."

"Some party," muttered the Chief. "Why don't you interview the boyfriend?" he suggested to Chase. "I'll have a look around the house." He turned to Odelia. "And you… why don't you do what you do best?"

She nodded her understanding. Uncle Alec was one of the few people in the world who knew about her ability to talk to cats, and with so many cats on the premises, there was a good chance one of them had seen something.

"And what is that, exactly?" asked Chase. "Snooping around?"

She gave him a thin-lipped smile. "That's right. I'm an ace snooper."

He shook his head, and muttered, "Unbelievable."

It was safe to say he wasn't a big fan of Uncle Alec's policy of including his niece in his investigations. But since he wasn't in charge, there was nothing he could do but grumble.

She passed into the house, in search of the cats, and found about a dozen of them looking glum and occupying couches and every other available surface in the family room. She took a seat to talk to them, but they merely stared at her with their sad eyes, and refused to acknowledge her presence.

Finally, she wandered on, hoping that Max and Dooley had had better luck. The house was just what you'd expect from a famous singer. At first glance, she saw a vintage guitar in a glass display case, and knew it was the guitar that had been on the cover of his first hit record. Huge portraits of the man were everywhere, looking as he did in his prime. This wasn't the house of a mere mortal, but a genuine star.

She arrived in the hallway, with its sweeping staircase, and wondered where Max and Dooley could be. The house was so big it was easy to get lost. She decided to venture upstairs and see if her cats were there. Ascending the stairs, she was careful not to touch anything, knowing the crime scene people would want to check the entire place for fingerprints.

Arriving on the landing, she saw several doors leading off the central hallway, and wondered how many rooms there could possibly be in this place. Every door sported an enlarged laminated reproduction of one of his album covers. For a moment, she stood poised, wondering where to start. Then, suddenly, she thought she heard a noise. It seemed to be coming from one of the rooms behind her so she turned and walked over. The door was ajar so she gently pushed it open with her elbow, and peered inside.

The first thing she saw was a huge multi-colored cockatoo, staring back at her from its perch in front of the window. So that explained the sound. And as she entered the room, she saw this was probably the master bedroom, as it was easily as large as a single floor of her own house. At the center of the room stood a large heart-shaped bed, with mirrored ceiling, and on this bed, she saw, rested the naked form of a very well-endowed young man.

He was fast asleep, in spite of the mutterings of the cockatoo, but then the large parrot reared up, spread its wings and took flight, screaming, "Come here, pretty boy! Come to Papa! Come to Papa right now, pretty boy!"

The young man suddenly jerked up, caught sight of Odelia, and started screaming, scrambling back against the wall, where a giant portrait of John Paul George had been placed, completely in the nude and looking buff.

"It's all right!" Odelia yelled, holding up her hands. "I'm a friend!"

But this didn't seem to console the young man, who looked like a male model, and was absolutely out of it. Probably still high from last night, she guessed, for his pupils were extremely dilated, and he seemed berserk.

He was probably one of last night's guests, and perhaps the last person to see the singer alive. His screams, meanwhile, carried through the open window and down to the pool area, and already she could hear footsteps pounding up the stairs. Moments later, Chase burst into the room, his eyes flying to the naked man on the bed. Then he caught sight of Odelia and shook his head. "I leave you alone for five minutes..."

The guy, taking a good look at Chase, now stopped

screaming. "Hey!" he shouted, suddenly looking disgruntled. "What the hell are you doing here?"

"I…" Chase began, but didn't get the chance to continue.

"Were you with Johnny just now? Don't you know the rules, man?"

"What rules?" Chase asked with a frown. "What are you talking about?"

"The rules, man! The one selected by Johnny stays." He then slapped his sculpted chest. "I was selected, buddy. I get to stay. Not you. Me! I'm the one who gets paid the big bucks. So why don't you get the hell out of here?!"

"Wowowow," said Chase, finally grasping the man's meaning.

"He thinks you're an escort, Chase," said Odelia helpfully.

"Hey!" cried Chase. "I'm not… No way can you even think that I'm…"

"You're a pretty boy," said the escort. "But I'm prettier. Now beat it."

"Yes, pretty boy Chase," Odelia said. "You weren't chosen, so beat it."

"You, too, lady," said the escort. "Johnny's not into bony bitches, or any bitches, for that matter, so get the hell out of here or I'll tell the agency."

Now it was Odelia's turn to glare at the guy. "I'm not bony!"

"You're practically a stick figure," said the escort. He was right about one thing, though, and so was the cockatoo. He really was a very pretty boy.

"Look, I'm not an escort, all right?" said Chase. "I'm a cop."

"That's great. Who cares? Cops, firemen, construction workers. Johnny's tastes run the gamut. But this time he chose a college professor. Me!"

"You're a college professor?" asked Odelia.

The guy planted his hands on his narrow hips. "Don't I look like a college professor to you?"

"Not like any college professors I've ever seen," she said, remembering her own college days. The professors had all been woolly-headed hobbits. Maybe if they'd looked more like this guy she'd have paid attention.

"I don't care! I was chosen! Johnny chose me! Me! Me! Me!"

At this point, Chase must have had enough, for he suddenly pulled his gun, and pointed it at the self-declared college professor. "Hands up!"

"Oh, now you're talking," said the guy, still pretty hyped-up. "Are you gonna shoot me, cop? Are you going to take a shot at me?! Catch me if you can!"

And with these words, he hopped from the bed and before either Odelia or Chase could stop him, jumped out the window!

They both hurried over and stared down. The naked college professor lay sprawled on what had been JPG's terrace table, which had collapsed when he'd taken a running leap at it. Two uniformed officers leaned over him.

"Is he dead?" yelled Chase.

One of them looked up. "Nope."

"Too bad," grunted Chase, holstering his weapon.

And as both he and Odelia headed down, she said, "You could be an escort, you know, pretty boy."

He gave her a grin, which was the first time today. "Good to know I've got a backup career plan in case my days as a cop are over." Then he gave her a quick once-over. "And for your information, you're not bony at all."

"Thanks," she said, and felt a blush creep up her cheeks.

Just then, the cockatoo decided to join them. Shouting,

"Come here, pretty boy!" he swung down and landed on Chase's shoulder. "Come to Papa!"

"Christ," growled Chase. "I hate this case already."

ABOUT NIC

Nic has a background in political science and before being struck by the writing bug worked odd jobs around the world (including but not limited to massage therapist in Mexico, gardener in Italy, restaurant manager in India, and Berlitz teacher in Belgium).

When he's not writing he enjoys curling up with a good (comic) book, watching British crime dramas, French comedies or Nancy Meyers movies, sampling pastry (apple cake!), pasta and chocolate (preferably the dark variety), twisting himself into a pretzel doing morning yoga, going for a brisk walk, and spoiling his feline assistants Lily and Ricky.

He lives with his wife (and aforementioned cats) in a small village smack dab in the middle of absolutely nowhere and is probably writing his next 'Mysteries of Max' book right now.

www.nicsaint.com

Made in the USA
Las Vegas, NV
24 August 2024

94292288R10132